Carl van Vechten

Lords of the Housetops

Thirteen Cat Tales

CLASSIC PAGES

Carl van Vechten

Lords of the Housetops

Thirteen Cat Tales

Reihe: classic pages

1. Auflage 2010 | ISBN: 978-3-86741-501-9

© Europäischer Hochschulverlag GmbH & Co KG

www.classic-pages.de

PREFACE

In the essay and especially in poetry the cat has become a favourite subject, but in fiction it must be admitted that he lags considerably behind the dog. The reasons for this apparently arbitrary preference on the part of authors are perfectly easy to explain. The instinctive acts of the dog, who is a company-loving brute, are very human; his psychology on occasion is almost human. He often behaves as a man would behave. It is therefore a comparatively simple matter to insert a dog into a story about men, for he can often carry it along after the fashion of a human character.

But, as Andrew Lang has so well observed, literature can never take a thing simply for what it is worth. "The plain-dealing dog must be distinctly bored by the ever-growing obligation to live up to the anecdotes of him.... These anecdotes are not told for his sake; they are told to save the self-respect of people who want an idol, and who are distorting him into a figure of pure convention for their domestic altars. He is now expected to discriminate between relations and mere friends of the house; to wag his tail at *God Save the Queen*; to count up to five in chips of fire-wood, and to seven in mutton bones; to howl for all deaths in the family above the degree of second cousin; to post letters, and refuse them when they have been insufficiently stamped; and last, and most intolerable, to show a tender solicitude when tabby is out of sorts." The dog, indeed, for the most part, has become as sentimental and conventional a figure in current fiction as the ghost who haunts the ouija board or the idealistic soldier returned from the wars to reconstruct his own country.

Now the cat, independent, liberty-loving, graceful, strong, resourceful, dignified, and self-respecting, has a psychology essentially feline, which has few points of contact with human psychology. The cat does not rescue babies from drowning or say his prayers in real life; consequently any attempt to make him do so in fiction would be ridiculous. He has, to be sure, his own virtues. To me these are considerably greater than those of any other animal. But the fact remains that the satisfactory treatment of the cat in fiction requires not only a deep knowledge of but also a deep affection for the sphinx of the fireside. Even then the difficulties can only be met in part, for the novelist must devise a situation in which human and feline psychology can be merged. The Egyptians probably could have written good cat stories. Perhaps they did. I sometimes ponder over the possibility of a cat room having been destroyed in the celebrated holocaust of Alexandria. The folk and fairy tales devoted to the cat, of which there are many, are based on an understanding, although often superficial, of cat traits. But the moderns, speaking generally, have not been able to do justice, in the novel or the short story, to this occult and lovable little beast.

On the whole, however, the stories I have chosen for this volume meet the test fairly well. Other cat stories exist, scores of them, but these, with one or two exceptions, are the best I know. In some instances other stories with very similar subjects might have been substituted, for each story in this book has been included for some special reason. Mrs. Freeman's story is a subtle symbolic treatment of the theme. In *The Blue Dryad* the cat is exhibited in his useful capacity as a killer of vermin. *A Psychical Invasion* is a successful attempt to exploit the undoubted occult powers of the cat. Poe's famous tale paints puss as an avenger of wrongs. In *Zut* the often inexplicable desire of the cat to change his home has a charming setting. Booth Tarkington in *Gipsy* has made a brilliant study of a wild city cat, living his own independent life with no apparent means of support. I should state that the ending of the story, which is a chapter from *Penrod and Sam*, is purely arbitrary. Gipsy, you will be glad to learn, was not drowned. He never would be. If you care to read the rest of his history you must turn to the book from which this excerpt was torn. There seem to be three excellent reasons for including Mark Twain's amusing skit: in the first place it is distinctly entertaining; in the second place Mr. Clemens adored cats to such an extent that it would be impertinent to publish a book of cat stories without including something from his pen; in the third place *Dick Baker's Cat* [1] celebrates an exceedingly important feline trait, the inability to be duped twice by the same phenomenon. It is interesting to record that Theodore Roosevelt liked this yarn so much that he named a White House cat, Tom Quartz.

[1] Those who have attempted to form anthologies or collections of stories similar to this know what difficulties have to be overcome. The publishers of Mark Twain's works were at first unwilling to grant me permission to use this story. I wish here to take occasion to thank Mrs. Clara Clemens Gabrilowitsch and Mr. Albert Bigelow Paine for their successful efforts in my behalf. I am sure that the readers of this book will be equally grateful.

Thomas A. Janvier's narrative reveals the cat in his luxurious capacity as a treasured pet, and Mr. Alden's story is a good example of the kind of tale in which a friendless human being depends upon an animal for affection. There are, of course, many such, but in most cases dogs are the heroes. *The Queen's Cat* is a story about an ailurophobe, or a cat-fearer, and his cure. Mr. Hudson's contribution is fact rather than fiction. I have included it because it is delightful and because it is the only good example available of that sort of story in which a cat becomes friendly with a member of an enemy race, although in life the thing is common. Mr. Warner's *Calvin*, too, certainly is not fiction, but as it shares with Pierre Loti's *Vies de deux chattes* the distinction of being one of the two best cat biographies that have yet been written I could not omit it.

There remains *The Afflictions of an English Cat* which, it will be perceived by even a careless reader, is certainly a good deal more than a cat story. It is, indeed, a satire on British respectability, but we Americans of today need not snicker at the English while reading it, for the point is equally applicable to us. When I first run across this tale while preparing material for my long cat book, *The Tiger in the House*, I was immensely amused, and to my great astonishment I have not been able to find an English translation of it. The story, the original title of which is *Peines de cœur d'une chatte anglaise*, first appeared in a volume of satires called *Scènes de la vie privée et publique des animaux*, issued by Hetzel in Paris in 1846, and to which George Sand, Alfred de Musset, and others contributed. The main purpose of the collaboration was doubtless to furnish a text to the extraordinary drawings of Grandville, who had an uncanny talent for merging human and animal characteristics. The volume was translated into English by J. Thompson and published in London in 1877, but for obvious reasons *The Afflictions of an English Cat* was not included in the translation, although Balzac's name would have added lustre to the collection. But in the Victorian age such a rough satire would scarcely have been tolerated. Even in French the story is not easily accessible. Aside from its original setting I have found it in but one edition of Balzac, the *Œuvres Complètes* issued in de luxe form by Calmann-Levy in 1879, where it is buried in the twenty-first volume, *Œuvres Diverses*.

Therefore I make no excuse for translating and offering it to my readers, for although perhaps it was not intended for a picture of cat life, the observation on the whole is true enough, and the story itself is too delicious to pass by. I should state that the opening and closing paragraphs refer to earlier chapters in the *Vie privée et publique des animaux*. I have, I may add, omitted one or two brief passages out of consideration for what is called American taste.

Carl Van Vechten.

April 6, 1920.
New York.

CONTENTS

Mary E. Wilkins Freeman: THE CAT   1

Guy Wetmore Carryl: ZUT   9

Algernon Blackwood: A PSYCHICAL INVASION   22

Honoré de Balzac: THE AFFLICTIONS OF AN ENGLISH
CAT   79

Booth Tarkington: GIPSY   94

G. H. Powell: THE BLUE DRYAD   99

Mark Twain: DICK BAKER'S CAT   109

Edgar Allan Poe: THE BLACK CAT   112

Thomas A. Janvier: MADAME JOLICŒUR'S CAT   122

W. H. Hudson: A FRIENDLY RAT   148

William Livingston Alden: MONTY'S FRIEND   152

Peggy Bacon: THE QUEEN'S CAT   165

Charles Dudley Warner: CALVIN   169

THE CAT

The snow was falling, and the Cat's fur was stiffly pointed with it, but he was imperturbable. He sat crouched, ready for the death-spring, as he had sat for hours. It was night — but that made no difference — all times were as one to the Cat when he was in wait for prey. Then, too, he was under no constraint of human will, for he was living alone that winter. Nowhere in the world was any voice calling him; on no hearth was there a waiting dish. He was quite free except for his own desires, which tyrannized over him when unsatisfied as now. The Cat was very hungry — almost famished, in fact. For days the weather had been very bitter, and all the feebler wild things which were his prey by inheritance, the born serfs to his family, had kept, for the most part, in their burrows and nests, and the Cat's long hunt had availed him nothing. But he waited with the inconceivable patience and persistency of his race; besides, he was certain. The Cat was a creature of absolute convictions, and his faith in his deductions never wavered. The rabbit had gone in there between those low-hung pine boughs. Now her little doorway had before it a shaggy curtain of snow, but in there she was. The Cat had seen her enter, so like a swift grey shadow that even his sharp and practised eyes had glanced back for the substance following, and then she was gone. So he sat down and waited, and he waited still in the white night, listening angrily to the north wind starting in the upper heights of the mountains with distant screams, then swelling into an awful crescendo of rage, and swooping down with furious white wings of snow like a flock of fierce eagles into the valleys and ravines. The Cat was on the side of a mountain, on a wooded terrace. Above him a few feet away towered the rock ascent as steep as the wall of a cathedral. The Cat had never climbed it — trees were the ladders to his heights of life. He had often looked with wonder at the rock, and miauled bitterly and resentfully as man does in the face of a forbidding Providence. At his left was the sheer precipice. Behind him, with a short stretch of woody growth between, was the frozen perpendicular wall of a mountain stream. Before him was the way to his home. When the rabbit came out she was trapped; her little cloven feet could

1

not scale such unbroken steeps. So the Cat waited. The place in which he was looked like a maelstrom of the wood. The tangle of trees and bushes clinging to the mountain-side with a stern clutch of roots, the prostrate trunks and branches, the vines embracing everything with strong knots and coils of growth, had a curious effect, as of things which had whirled for ages in a current of raging water, only it was not water, but wind, which had disposed everything in circling lines of yielding to its fiercest points of onset. And now over all this whirl of wood and rock and dead trunks and branches and vines descended the snow. It blew down like smoke over the rock-crest above; it stood in a gyrating column like some death-wraith of nature, on the level, then it broke over the edge of the precipice, and the Cat cowered before the fierce backward set of it. It was as if ice needles pricked his skin through his beautiful thick fur, but he never faltered and never once cried. He had nothing to gain from crying, and everything to lose; the rabbit would hear him cry and know he was waiting.

It grew darker and darker, with a strange white smother, instead of the natural blackness of night. It was a night of storm and death superadded to the night of nature. The mountains were all hidden, wrapped about, overawed, and tumultuously overborne by it, but in the midst of it waited, quite unconquered, this little, unswerving, living patience and power under a little coat of grey fur.

A fiercer blast swept over the rock, spun on one mighty foot of whirlwind athwart the level, then was over the precipice.

Then the Cat saw two eyes luminous with terror, frantic with the impulse of flight, he saw a little, quivering, dilating nose, he saw two pointing ears, and he kept still, with every one of his fine nerves and muscles strained like wires. Then the rabbit was out — there was one long line of incarnate flight and terror — and the Cat had her.

Then the Cat went home, trailing his prey through the snow.

The Cat lived in the house which his master had built, as rudely as a child's block-house, but stanchly enough. The snow was heavy on the low slant of its roof, but it would not settle under it. The two windows and the door were made fast, but the Cat knew a way in. Up a pine-tree behind the house he scuttled, though it was hard work with his heavy rabbit, and was in his little window under the eaves, then down through the trap to the room below, and on his master's bed with a spring and a great cry of triumph, rabbit and all. But his master was not there; he had been gone since early fall and it was now February. He would not return until spring, for he was an old man, and the cruel cold of the mountains clutched at his vitals like a panther, and he had gone to the village to winter. The Cat had known for a long time that his master was gone, but his reasoning was always sequential and circuitous; always for him what had been would be, and the more easily for his marvellous waiting powers so he always came home expecting to find his master.

When he saw that he was still gone, he dragged the rabbit off the rude couch which was the bed to the floor, put one little paw on the carcass to keep it steady, and began gnawing with head to one side to bring his strongest teeth to bear.

It was darker in the house than it had been in the wood, and the cold was as deadly, though not so fierce. If the Cat had not received his fur coat unquestioningly of Providence, he would have been thankful that he had it. It was a mottled grey, white on the face and breast, and thick as fur could grow.

The wind drove the snow on the windows with such force that it rattled like sleet, and the house trembled a little. Then all at once the Cat heard a noise, and stopped gnawing his rabbit and listened, his shining green eyes fixed upon a window. Then he heard a hoarse shout, a halloo of despair and entreaty; but he knew it was not his master come home, and he waited, one paw still on the rabbit. Then the halloo came again, and then the Cat answered. He said all that was essential quite plainly to his own comprehension. There was in his cry of response inquiry, information, warning, terror, and finally, the offer of comradeship; but the man outside did not hear him, because of the howling of the storm.

Then there was a great battering pound at the door, then another, and another. The Cat dragged his rabbit under the bed. The blows came thicker and faster. It was a weak arm which gave them, but it was nerved by desperation. Finally the lock yielded, and the stranger came in. Then the Cat, peering from under the bed, blinked with a sudden light, and his green eyes narrowed. The stranger struck a match and looked about. The Cat saw a face wild and blue with hunger and cold, and a man who looked poorer and older than his poor old master, who was an outcast among men for his poverty and lowly mystery of antecedents; and he heard a muttered, unintelligible voicing of distress from the harsh piteous mouth. There was in it both profanity and prayer, but the Cat knew nothing of that.

The stranger braced the door which he had forced, got some wood from the stock in the corner, and kindled a fire in the old stove as quickly as his half-frozen hands would allow. He shook so pitiably as he worked that the Cat under the bed felt the tremor of it. Then the man, who was small and feeble and marked with the scars of suffering which he had pulled down upon his own head, sat down in one of the old chairs and crouched over the fire as if it were the one love and desire of his soul, holding out his yellow hands like yellow claws, and he groaned. The Cat came out from under the bed and leaped up on his lap with the rabbit. The man gave a great shout and start of terror, and sprang, and the Cat slid clawing to the floor, and the rabbit fell inertly, and the man leaned, gasping with fright, and ghastly, against the wall. The Cat grabbed the rabbit by the slack of its neck and dragged it to the man's feet. Then he raised his shrill, insistent cry, he arched his back high, his tail was a splendid waving plume. He rubbed against the man's feet, which were bursting out of their torn shoes.

The man pushed the Cat away, gently enough, and began searching about the little cabin. He even climbed painfully the ladder to the loft, lit a match, and peered up in the darkness with straining eyes. He feared lest there might be a man, since there was a cat. His experience with men had not been pleasant, and neither had the experience of men been pleasant with him. He

4

was an old wandering Ishmael among his kind; he had stumbled upon the house of a brother, and the brother was not at home, and he was glad.

He returned to the Cat, and stooped stiffly and stroked his back, which the animal arched like the spring of a bow.

Then he took up the rabbit and looked at it eagerly by the firelight. His jaws worked. He could almost have devoured it raw. He fumbled — the Cat close at his heels — around some rude shelves and a table, and found, with a grunt of self-gratulation, a lamp with oil in it. That he lighted; then he found a frying-pan and a knife, and skinned the rabbit, and prepared it for cooking, the Cat always at his feet.

When the odour of the cooking flesh filled the cabin, both the man and the Cat looked wolfish. The man turned the rabbit with one hand and stooped to pat the Cat with the other. The Cat thought him a fine man. He loved him with all his heart, though he had known him such a short time, and though the man had a face both pitiful and sharply set at variance with the best of things.

It was a face with the grimy grizzle of age upon it, with fever hollows in the cheeks, and the memories of wrong in the dim eyes, but the Cat accepted the man unquestioningly and loved him. When the rabbit was half cooked, neither the man nor the Cat could wait any longer. The man took it from the fire, divided it exactly in halves, gave the Cat one, and took the other himself. Then they ate.

Then the man blew out the light, called the Cat to him, got on the bed, drew up the ragged coverings, and fell asleep with the Cat in his bosom.

The man was the Cat's guest all the rest of the winter, and winter is long in the mountains. The rightful owner of the little hut did not return until May. All that time the Cat toiled hard, and he grew rather thin himself, for he shared everything except mice with his guest; and sometimes game was wary, and the fruit of patience of days was very little for two. The man was ill and weak, however, and unable to eat much, which was fortunate, since he could not hunt for himself. All day long he lay on the bed, or else sat crouched over the fire. It was a good thing that fire-wood was ready at hand for the picking up, not a stone's-throw from the door, for that he had to attend to himself.

The Cat foraged tirelessly. Sometimes he was gone for days together, and at first the man used to be terrified, thinking he would never return; then he would hear the familiar cry at the door, and stumble to his feet and let him in. Then the two would dine together, sharing equally; then the Cat would rest and purr, and finally sleep in the man's arms.

Towards spring the game grew plentiful; more wild little quarry were tempted out of their homes, in search of love as well as food. One day the Cat had luck — a rabbit, a partridge, and a mouse. He could not carry them all at once, but finally he had them together at the house door. Then he cried, but no one answered. All the mountain streams were loosened, and the air was full of the gurgle of many waters, occasionally pierced by a bird-whistle. The trees rustled with a new sound to the spring wind; there was a flush of rose and gold-green on the breasting surface of a distant mountain seen through an opening in the wood. The tips of the bushes were swollen and glistening red, and now and then there was a flower; but the Cat had nothing to do with flowers. He stood beside his booty at the house door, and cried and cried with his insistent triumph and complaint and pleading, but no one came to let him in. Then the cat left his little treasures at the door, and went around to the back of the house to the pine-tree, and was up the trunk with a wild scramble, and in through his little window, and down through the trap to the room, and the man was gone.

The Cat cried again — that cry of the animal for human companionship which is one of the sad notes of the world; he looked in all the corners; he sprang to the chair at the window and looked out; but no one came. The man was gone and he never came again.

The Cat ate his mouse out on the turf beside the house; the

rabbit and the partridge he carried painfully into the house, but the man did not come to share them. Finally, in the course of a day or two, he ate them up himself; then he slept a long time on the bed, and when he waked the man was not there.

Then the Cat went forth to his hunting-grounds again, and came home at night with a plump bird, reasoning with his tireless persistency in expectancy that the man would be there; and there was a light in the window, and when he cried his old master opened the door and let him in.

His master had strong comradeship with the Cat, but not affection. He never patted him like that gentler outcast, but he had a pride in him and an anxiety for his welfare, though he had left him alone all winter without scruple. He feared lest some misfortune might have come to the Cat, though he was so large of his kind, and a mighty hunter. Therefore, when he saw him at the door in all the glory of his glossy winter coat, his white breast and face shining like snow in the sun, his own face lit up with welcome, and the Cat embraced his feet with his sinuous body vibrant with rejoicing purrs.

The Cat had his bird to himself, for his master had his own supper already cooking on the stove. After supper the Cat's master took his pipe, and sought a small store of tobacco which he had left in his hut over winter. He had thought often of it; that and the Cat seemed something to come home to in the spring. But the tobacco was gone; not a dust left. The man swore a little in a grim monotone, which made the profanity lose its customary effect. He had been, and was, a hard drinker; he had knocked about the world until the marks of its sharp corners were on his very soul, which was thereby calloused, until his very sensibility to loss was dulled. He was a very old man.

He searched for the tobacco with a sort of dull combativeness of persistency; then he stared with stupid wonder around the room. Suddenly many features struck him as being changed. Another stove-lid was broken; an old piece of carpet was tacked up over a window to keep out the cold; his fire-wood was gone. He looked and there was no oil left in his can. He looked at the coverings on his bed; he took them up, and again he made that strange remonstrant noise in his throat. Then he looked again for his tobacco.

Finally he gave it up. He sat down beside the fire, for May in the mountains is cold; he held his empty pipe in his mouth, his rough forehead knitted, and he and the Cat looked at each other across that impassable barrier of silence which has been set between man and beast from the creation of the world.

Mary E. Wilkins Freeman.

ZUT

Side by side, on the avenue de la Grande Armée, stand the épicerie of Jean-Baptiste Caille and the salle de coiffure of Hippolyte Sergeot, and between these two there is a great gulf fixed, the which has come to be through the acerbity of Alexandrine Caille (according to Espérance Sergeot), though the duplicity of Espérance Sergeot (according to Alexandrine Caille). But the veritable root of all evil is Zut, and Zut sits smiling in Jean-Baptiste's doorway, and cares naught for anything in the world, save the sunlight and her midday meal.

When Hippolyte found himself in a position to purchase the salle de coiffure, he gave evidence of marked acumen by uniting himself in the holy — and civil — bonds of matrimony with the retiring patron's daughter, whose dot ran into the coveted five figures, and whose heart, said Hippolyte, was as good as her face was pretty, which, even by the unprejudiced, was acknowledged to be forcible commendation. The installation of the new establishment was a nine days' wonder in the quartier. It is a busy thoroughfare at its western end, is the avenue de la Grande Armée, crowded with bicyclists and with a multitude of creatures fearfully and wonderfully clad, who do incomprehensible things in connection with motor-carriages. Also there are big cafés in plenty, whose waiters must be smoothly shaven: and moreover, at the time when Hippolyte came into his own, the porte Maillot station of the Métropolitain had already pushed its entrée and sortie up through the soil, not a hundred metres from his door, where they stood like atrocious yellow tulips, art nouveau, breathing people out and in by thousands. There was no lack of possible custom. The problem was to turn possible into probable, and probable into permanent; and here the seven wits and the ten thousand francs of Espérance came prominently to the fore. She it was who sounded the progressive note, which is half the secret of success.

"Pour attirer les gens," she said, with her arms akimbo, "il faut d'abord les épater."

In her creed all that was worth doing at all was worth doing gloriously. So, under her guidance, Hippolyte journeyed from shop to shop in the faubourg St. Antoine, and spent hours of impassioned argument with carpenters and decorators. In the end, the salle de coiffure was glorified by fresh paint without and within, and by the addition of a long mirror in a gilt frame, and a complicated apparatus of gleaming nickel-plate, which went by the imposing title of appareil antiseptique, and the acquisition of which was duly proclaimed by a special placard that swung at right angles to the door. The shop was rechristened, too, and the black and white sign across its front which formerly bore the simple inscription "Kilbert, Coiffeur," now blazoned abroad the vastly more impressive legend "Salon Malakoff." The window shelves fairly groaned beneath their burden of soaps, toilet waters, and perfumery, a string of bright yellow sponges occupied each corner of the window, and, through the agency of white enamel letters on the pane itself, public attention was drawn to the apparently contradictory facts that English was spoken and "schampoing" given within. Then Hippolyte engaged two assistants, and clad them in white duck jackets, and his wife fabricated a new blouse of blue silk, and seated herself behind the desk with an engaging smile. The enterprise was fairly launched, and experience was not slow in proving the theories of Espérance to be well founded. The quartier was épaté from the start, and took with enthusiasm the bait held forth. The affairs of the Salon Malakoff prospered prodigiously.

But there is a serpent in every Eden, and in that of the Sergeot this rôle was assumed by Alexandrine Caille. The worthy épicier himself was of too torpid a temperament to fall a victim to the gnawing tooth of envy, but in the soul of his wife the launch, and, what was worse, the immediate prosperity of the Salon Malakoff, bred dire resentment. Her own establishment had grown grimy with the passage of time, and the annual profits displayed a constant and disturbing tendency toward complete evaporation, since the coming of the big cafés, and the resultant subversion of custom to the wholesale dealers. This persistent narrowing of the former appreciable gap between purchase and selling price rankled in Alexandrine's mind, but her misguided efforts to maintain the percentage of profit by recourse to inferior qualities only made bad worse, and, even as the Sergeot were steering the Salon Malakoff forth upon the waters of prosperity, there were nightly conferences in the household next door, at which impending ruin presided, and exasperation sounded the keynote of every sentence. The resplendent façade of Hippolyte's establishment, the tide of custom which poured into and out of his door, the loudly expressed admiration of his ability and thrift, which greeted her ears on every side, and, finally, the sight of Espérance, fresh, smiling, and prosperous, behind her little counter — all these were as gall and wormwood to Alexandrine, brooding over her accumulating debts and her decreasing earnings, among her dusty stacks of jars and boxes. Once she had called upon her neighbour, somewhat for courtesy's sake, but more for curiosity's, and since then the agreeable scent of violet and lilac perfumery dwelt always in her memory, and mirages of scrupulously polished nickel and glass hung always before her eyes. The air of her own shop was heavy with the pungent odours of raw vegetables, cheeses, and dried fish, and no brilliance redeemed the sardine and biscuit boxes which surrounded her. Life became a bitter thing to Alexandrine Caille, for if nothing is more gratifying than one's own success, surely nothing is less so than that of one's neighbour. Moreover, her visit had never been returned, and this again was fuel for her rage.

But the sharpest thorn in her flesh — and even in that of her phlegmatic husband — was the base desertion to the enemy's camp of Abel Flique. In the days when Madame Caille was unmarried, and when her ninety kilos were fifty still, Abel had been youngest commis in the very shop over which she now held sway, and the most devoted suitor in all her train. Even after his prowess in the black days of '71 had won him the attention of the civil authorities, and a grateful municipality had transformed the grocer-soldier into a guardian of law and order, he still hung upon the favour of his heart's first love, and only gave up the struggle when Jean-Baptiste bore off the prize and enthroned her in state as presiding genius of his newly acquired épicerie. Later, an unwittingly kindly prefect had transferred Abel to the seventeenth arrondissement, and so the old friendship was picked up where it had been dropped, and the ruddy-faced agent found it both convenient and agreeable to drop in frequently at Madame Caille's on his way home, and exchange a few words of reminiscence or banter for a box of sardines or a minute package of tea. But, with the deterioration in his old friends' wares, and the almost simultaneous appearance of the Salon Malakoff, his loyalty wavered. Flique sampled the advantages of Hippolyte's establishment, and, being won over thereby, returned again and again. His hearty laugh came to be heard almost daily in the salle de coiffure, and because he was a brave homme and a good customer, who did not stand upon a question of a few sous, but allowed Hippolyte to work his will, and trim and curl and perfume him to his heart's content, there was always a welcome for him, and a smile from Madame Sergeot, and occasionally a little present of brillantine or perfumery, for friendship's sake, and because it is well to have the good-will of the all-powerful police.

From her window Madame Caille observed the comings and goings of Abel with a resentful eye. It was rarely now that he glanced into the épicerie as he passed, and still more rarely that he greeted his former flame with a stiff nod. Once she had hailed him from the doorway, sardines in hand, but he had replied that he was pressed for time, and had passed rapidly on. Then indeed did blackness descend upon the soul of Alexandrine, and in her deepest consciousness she vowed to have revenge. Neither the occasion nor the method was as yet clear to her, but she pursed her lips ominously, and bided her time.

In the existence of Madame Caille there was one emphatic consolation for all misfortunes, the which was none other than Zut, a white angora cat of surpassing beauty and prodigious size. She had come into Alexandrine's possession as a kitten, and, what with much eating and an inherent distaste for exercise, had attained her present proportions and her superb air of unconcern. It was from the latter that she derived her name, the which, in Parisian argot, at once means everything and nothing, but is chiefly taken to signify complete and magnificent indifference to all things mundane and material: and in the matter of indifference Zut was past-mistress. Even for Madame Caille herself, who fed her with the choicest morsels from her own plate, brushed her fine fur with excessive care, and addressed caressing remarks to her at minute intervals throughout the day, Zut manifested a lack of interest that amounted to contempt. As she basked in the warm sun at the shop door, the round face of her mistress beamed upon her from the little desk, and the voice of her mistress sent fulsome flattery winging toward her on the heavy air. Was she beautiful, mon Dieu! In effect, all that one could dream of the most beautiful! And her eyes, of a blue like the heaven, were they not wise and calm? Mon Dieu, yes! It was a cat among thousands, a mimi almost divine.

Jean-Baptiste, appealed to for confirmation of these statements, replied that it was so. There was no denying that this was a magnificent beast. And of a chic. And caressing — (which was exaggeration). And of an affection — (which was doubtful). And courageous — (which was wholly untrue). Mazette, yes! A cat of cats! And was the boy to be the whole afternoon in delivering a cheese, he demanded of her? And Madame Caille would challenge him to ask her that — but it was a good, great beast all the same! — and so bury herself again in her accounts, until her attention was once more drawn to Zut, and fresh flattery poured forth. For all of this Zut cared less than nothing. In the midst of her mistress's sweetest cajolery, she simply closed her sapphire eyes, with an inexpressibly eloquent air of weariness, or turned to the intricacies of her toilet, as who should say: "Continue. I am listening. But it is unimportant."

But long familiarity with her disdain had deprived it of any sting, so far as Alexandrine was concerned. Passive indifference she could suffer. It was only when Zut proceeded to an active manifestation of ingratitude that she inflicted an irremediable wound. Returning from her marketing one morning, Madame Caille discovered her graceless favourite seated complacently in the doorway of the Salon Malakoff, and, in a paroxysm of indignation, bore down upon her, and snatched her to her breast.

"Unhappy one!" she cried, planting herself in full view of Espérance, and, while raining the letter of her reproach upon the truant, contriving to apply its spirit wholly to her neighbour. "What hast thou done? Is it that thou desertest me for strangers, who may destroy thee? Name of a name, hast thou no heart? They would steal thee from me — and above all, *now*! Well then, no! One shall see if such things are permitted! Vagabond!" And with this parting shot, which passed harmlessly over the head of the offender, and launched itself full at Madame Sergeot, the outraged épicière flounced back into her own domain, where, turning, she threatened the empty air with a passionate gesture.

"Vagabond!" she repeated. "Good-for-nothing! Is it not enough to have robbed me of my friends, that you must steal my child as well? We shall see!" — then, suddenly softening — "Thou art beautiful, and good, and wise. Mon Dieu, if I should lose thee, and above all, *now*!"

Now there existed a marked, if unvoiced, community of feeling between Espérance and her resentful neighbour, for the former's passion for cats was more consuming even than the latter's. She had long cherished the dream of possessing a white angora, and when, that morning, of her own accord, Zut stepped into the Salon Malakoff, she was received with demonstrations even warmer than those to which she had long since become accustomed. And, whether it was the novelty of her surroundings, or merely some unwonted instinct which made her unusually susceptible, her habitual indifference then and there gave place to animation, and her satisfaction was vented in her long, appreciative purr, wherewith it was not once a year that she vouchsafed to gladden her owner's heart. Espérance hastened to prepare a saucer of milk, and, when this was exhausted, added a generous portion of fish, and Zut then made a tour of the shop, rubbing herself against the chair-legs, and receiving the homage of customers and duck-clad assistants alike. Flique, his ruddy face screwed into a mere knot of features, as Hippolyte worked violet hair-tonic into his brittle locks, was moved to satire by the apparition.

"Tiens! It is with the cat as with the clients. All the world forsakes the Caille."

Strangely enough, the wrathful words of Alexandrine, as she snatched her darling from the doorway, awoke in the mind of Espérance her first suspicion of this smouldering resentment.

Absorbed in the launching of her husband's affairs, and constantly employed in the making of change and with the keeping of her simple accounts, she had had no time to bestow upon her neighbours, and, even had her attention been free, she could hardly have been expected to deduce the rancour of Madame Caille from the evidence at hand. But even if she had been able to ignore the significance of that furious outburst at her very door, its meaning had not been lost upon the others, and her own half-formed conviction was speedily confirmed.

"What has she?" cried Hippolyte, pausing in the final stage of his operations upon the highly perfumed Flique.

"Do I know?" replied his wife with a shrug. "She thinks I stole her cat — *I*!"

"Quite simply, she hates you," put in Flique. "And why not? She is old, and fat, and her business is taking itself off, like that! You are young and" — with a bow, as he rose — "beautiful, and your affairs march to a marvel. She is jealous, c'est tout! It is a bad character, that."

"But, mon Dieu!" —

"But what does that say to you? Let her go her way, she and her cat. Au r'voir, 'sieurs, 'dame."

And, rattling a couple of sous into the little urn reserved for tips, the policeman took his departure, amid a chorus of "Merci, m'sieu', au r'voir, m'sieu'," from Hippolyte and his duck-clad aids.

But what he had said remained behind. All day Madame Sergeot pondered upon the incident of the morning and Abel Flique's comments thereupon, seeking out some more plausible reason for this hitherto unsuspected enmity than the mere contrast between her material conditions and those of Madame Caille seemed to her to afford. For, to a natural placidity of temperament, which manifested itself in a reluctance to incur the displeasure of any one, had been lately added in Espérance a shrewd commercial instinct, which told her that the fortunes of the Salon Malakoff might readily be imperilled by an unfriendly tongue. In the quartier, gossip spread quickly and took deep root. It was quite imaginably within the power of Madame Caille to circulate such rumours of Sergeot dishonesty as should draw their lately won custom from them and leave but empty chairs and discontent where now all was prosperity and satisfaction.

Suddenly there came to her the memory of that visit which she had never returned. Mon Dieu! and was not that reason enough? She, the youngest patronne in the quartier, to ignore deliberately the friendly call of a neighbour! At least it was not too late to make amends. So, when business lagged a little in the late afternoon, Madame Sergeot slipped from her desk, and, after a furtive touch to her hair, went in next door, to pour oil upon the troubled waters.

Madame Caille, throned at her counter, received her visitor with unexampled frigidity.

"Ah, it is you," she said. "You have come to make some purchases, no doubt."

"Eggs, madame," answered her visitor, disconcerted, but tactfully accepting the hint.

"The best quality — or — ?" demanded Alexandrine, with the suggestion of a sneer.

"The best, evidently, madame. Six, if you please. Spring weather at last, it would seem."

To this generality the other made no reply. Descending from her stool, she blew sharply into a small paper bag, thereby distending it into a miniature balloon, and began selecting the eggs from a basket, holding each one to the light, and then dusting it with exaggerated care before placing it in the bag. While she was thus employed Zut advanced from a secluded corner, and, stretching her fore legs slowly to their utmost length, greeted her acquaintance of the morning with a yawn. Finding in the cat an outlet for her embarrassment, Espérance made another effort to give the interview a friendly turn.

"He is beautiful, madame, your matou," she said.

"It is a female," replied Madame Caille, turning abruptly from the basket, "and she does not care for strangers."

This second snub was not calculated to encourage neighbourly overtures, but Madame Sergeot had felt herself to be in the wrong, and was not to be so readily repulsed.

"We do not see Monsieur Caille at the Salon Malakoff," she continued. "We should be enchanted" —

"My husband shaves himself," retorted Alexandrine, with renewed dignity.

"But his hair" — ventured Espérance.

"*I* cut it!" thundered her foe.

Here Madame Sergeot made a false move. She laughed. Then, in confusion, and striving, too late, to retrieve herself — "Pardon, madame," she added, "but it seems droll to me, that. After all, ten sous is a sum so small" —

"All the world, unfortunately," broke in Madame Caille, "has not the wherewithal to buy mirrors, and pay itself frescoes and appareils antiseptiques! The eggs are twenty-four sous — but we do not pride ourselves upon our eggs. Perhaps you had better seek them elsewhere for the future!"

For sole reply Madame Sergeot had recourse to her expressive shrug, and then laying two francs upon the counter, and gathering up the sous which Alexandrine rather hurled at than handed her, she took her way toward the door with all the dignity at her command. But Madame Caille, feeling her snub to have been insufficient, could not let her go without a final thrust.

"Perhaps your husband will be so amiable as to shampoo my cat!" she shouted. "She seems to like your 'Salon'!"

But Espérance, while for concord's sake inclined to tolerate all rudeness to herself, was not prepared to hear Hippolyte insulted, and so, wheeling at the doorway, flung all her resentment into two words.

"Mal élevée!"

"Gueuse!" screamed Alexandrine from the desk. And so they parted.

Now, even at this stage, an armed truce might still have been preserved, had Zut been content with the evil she had wrought, and not thought it incumbent upon her further to embitter a quarrel that was a very pretty quarrel as it stood. But, whether it was that the milk and fish of the Salon Malakoff lay sweeter upon her memory than any of the familiar dainties of the épicerie Caille, or that, by her unknowable feline instinct, she was irresistibly drawn toward the scent of violet and lilac brillantine, her first visit to the Sergeot was soon repeated, and from this visit other visits grew, until it was almost a daily occurrence for her to saunter slowly into the salle de coiffure, and there receive the food and homage which were rendered as her undisputed due. For, whatever was the bitterness of Espérance toward Madame Caille, no part thereof descended upon Zut. On the contrary, at each visit her heart was more drawn toward the sleek angora, and her desire but strengthened to possess her peer. But white angoras are a luxury, and an expensive one at that, and, however prosperous the Salon Malakoff might be, its proprietors were not as yet in a position to squander eighty francs upon a whim. So, until profits should mount higher, Madame Sergeot was forced to content herself with the voluntary visits of her neighbour's pet.

Madame Caille did not yield her rights of sovereignty without a struggle. On the occasion of Zut's third visit, she descended upon the Salon Malakoff, robed in wrath, and found the adored one contentedly feeding on fish in the very bosom of the family Sergeot. An appalling scene ensued.

"If," she stormed, crimson of countenance, and threatening Espérance with her fist, "if you *must* entice my cat from her home, at *least* I will thank you not to give her food. I provide all that is necessary; and, for the rest, how do I know what is in that saucer?"

And she surveyed the duck-clad assistants and the astounded customers with tremendous scorn.

"You others," she added, "I ask you, is it just? These people take my cat, and feed her — *feed* her — with I know not what! It is overwhelming, unheard of — and, above all, *now!*"

But here the peaceful Hippolyte played trumps.

"It is the privilege of the vulgar," he cried, advancing, razor in hand, "when they are at home, to insult their neighbours, but here — no! My wife has told me of you and of your sayings. Beware! or I shall arrange your affair for you! Go! you and your cat!"

And, by way of emphasis, he fairly kicked Zut into her astonished owner's arms. He was magnificent, was Hippolyte!

This anecdote, duly elaborated, was poured into the ears of Abel Flique an hour later, and that evening he paid his first visit in many months to Madame Caille. She greeted him effusively, being willing to pardon all the past for the sake of regaining this powerful friend. But the glitter in the agent's eye would have cowed a fiercer spirit than hers.

"You amuse yourself," he said sternly, looking straight at her over the handful of raisins which she tendered him, "by wearying my friends. I counsel you to take care. One does not sell inferior eggs in Paris without hearing of it sooner or later. I know more than I have told, but not more than I *can* tell, if I choose."

"Our ancient friendship" — faltered Alexandrine, touched in a vulnerable spot.

" — preserves you thus far," added Flique, no less unmoved. "Beware how you abuse it!"

And so the calls of Zut were no longer disturbed.

But the rover spirit is progressive, and thus short visits became long visits, and finally the angora spent whole nights in the Salon Malakoff, where a box and a bit of carpet were provided for her. And one fateful morning the meaning of Madame Caille's significant words "and above all, *now!*" was made clear.

The prosperity of Hippolyte's establishment had grown apace, so that, on the morning in question, the three chairs were occupied, and yet other customers awaited their turn. The air was laden with violet and lilac. A stout chauffeur, in a leather suit, thickly coated with dust, was undergoing a shampoo at the hands of one of the duck-clad, and, under the skilfully plied razor of the other, the virgin down slid from the lips and chin of a slim and somewhat startled youth, while from a vaporizer Hippolyte played a fine spray of perfumed water upon the ruddy countenance of Abel Flique. It was an eloquent moment, eminently fitted for some dramatic incident, and that dramatic incident Zut supplied. She advanced slowly and with an air of conscious dignity from the corner where was her carpeted box, and in her mouth was a limp something, which, when deposited in the immediate centre of the Salon Malakoff, resolved itself into an angora kitten, as white as snow!

"Epatant!" said Flique, mopping his perfumed chin. And so it was.

There was an immediate investigation of Zut's quarters, which revealed four other kittens, but each of these was marked with black or tan. It was the flower of the flock with which the proud mother had won her public.

"And they are all yours!" cried Flique, when the question of ownership arose. "Mon Dieu, yes! There was such a case not a month ago, in the eighth arrondissement — a concierge of the avenue Hoche who made a contrary claim. But the courts decided against her. They are all yours, Madame Sergeot. My felicitations!"

Now, as we have said, Madame Sergeot was of a placid temperament which sought not strife. But the unprovoked insults of Madame Caille had struck deep, and, after all, she was but human.

So it was that, seated at her little desk, she composed the following masterpiece of satire:

Chère Madame, — We send you back your cat, and the others — all but one. One kitten was of a pure white, more beautiful even than its mother. As we have long desired a white angora, we keep this one as a souvenir of you. We regret that we do not see the means of accepting the kind offer you were so amiable as to make us. We fear that we shall not find time to shampoo your cat, as we shall be so busy taking care of our own. Monsieur Flique will explain the rest.

We pray you to accept, madame, the assurance of our distinguished consideration,

Hippolyte and Espérance Sergeot.

It was Abel Flique who conveyed the above epistle, and Zut, and four of Zut's kittens, to Alexandrine Caille, and, when that wrathful person would have rent him with tooth and nail, it was Abel Flique who laid his finger on his lip, and said, —

"Concern yourself with the superior kitten, madame, and I concern myself with the inferior eggs!"

To which Alexandrine made no reply. After Flique had taken his departure, she remained speechless for five consecutive minutes for the first time in the whole of her waking existence, gazing at the spot at her feet where sprawled the white angora, surrounded by her mottled offspring. Even when the first shock of her defeat had passed, she simply heaved a deep sigh, and uttered two words, —

"Oh, *Zut!*"

The which, in Parisian argot, at once means everything and nothing.

Guy Wetmore Carryl.

A PSYCHICAL INVASION

I

"And what is it makes you think I could be of use in this particular case?" asked Dr. John Silence, looking across somewhat sceptically at the Swedish lady in the chair facing him.

"Your sympathetic heart and your knowledge of occultism — "

"Oh, please — that dreadful word!" he interrupted, holding up a finger with a gesture of impatience.

"Well, then," she laughed, "your wonderful clairvoyant gift and your trained psychic knowledge of the processes by which a personality may be disintegrated and destroyed — these strange studies you've been experimenting with all these years — "

"If it's only a case of multiple personality I must really cry off," interrupted the doctor again hastily, a bored expression in his eyes.

"It's not that; now, please, be serious, for I want your help," she said; "and if I choose my words poorly you must be patient with my ignorance. The case I know will interest you, and no one else could deal with it so well. In fact, no ordinary professional man could deal with it at all, for I know of no treatment or medicine that can restore a lost sense of humour!"

"You begin to interest me with your 'case,'" he replied, and made himself comfortable to listen.

Mrs. Sivendson drew a sigh of contentment as she watched him go to the tube and heard him tell the servant he was not to be disturbed.

"I believe you have read my thoughts already," she said; "your intuitive knowledge of what goes on in other people's minds is positively uncanny."

Her friend shook his head and smiled as he drew his chair up to a convenient position and prepared to listen attentively to what she had to say. He closed his eyes, as he always did when he wished to absorb the real meaning of a recital that might be inadequately expressed, for by this method he found it easier to set himself in tune with the living thoughts that lay behind the broken words.

By his friends John Silence was regarded as an eccentric, because he was rich by accident, and by choice — a doctor. That a man of independent means should devote his time to doctoring, chiefly doctoring folk who could not pay, passed their comprehension entirely. The native nobility of a soul whose first desire was to help those who could not help themselves, puzzled them. After that, it irritated them, and, greatly to his own satisfaction, they left him to his own devices.

Dr. Silence was a free-lance, though, among doctors, having neither consulting-room, book-keeper, nor professional manner. He took no fees, being at heart a genuine philanthropist, yet at the same time did no harm to his fellow-practitioners, because he only accepted unremunerative cases, and cases that interested him for some very special reason. He argued that the rich could pay, and the very poor could avail themselves of organized charity, but that a very large class of ill-paid, self-respecting workers, often followers of the arts, could not afford the price of a week's comforts merely to be told to travel. And it was these he desired to help; cases often requiring special and patient study — things no doctor can give for a guinea, and that no one would dream of expecting him to give.

But there was another side to his personality and practice, and one with which we are now more directly concerned; for the cases that especially appealed to him were of no ordinary kind, but rather of that intangible, elusive, and difficult nature best described as psychical afflictions; and, though he would have been the last person himself to approve of the title, it was beyond question that he was known more or less generally as the "Psychic Doctor."

In order to grapple with cases of this peculiar kind, he had submitted himself to a long and severe training, at once physical, mental, and spiritual. What precisely this training had been, or where undergone, no one seemed to know, — for he never spoke of it, as, indeed, he betrayed no single other characteristic of the charlatan, — but the fact that it had involved a total disappearance from the world for five years, and that after he returned and began his singular practice no one ever dreamed of applying to him the so easily acquired epithet of quack, spoke much for the seriousness of his strange quest and also for the genuineness of his attainments.

For the modern psychical researcher he felt the calm tolerance of the "man who knows." There was a trace of pity in his voice — contempt he never showed — when he spoke of their methods.

"This classification of results is uninspired work at best," he said once to me, when I had been his confidential assistant for some years. "It leads nowhere, and after a hundred years will lead nowhere. It is playing with the wrong end of a rather dangerous toy. Far better, it would be, to examine the causes, and then the results would so easily slip into place and explain themselves. For the sources are accessible, and open to all who have the courage to lead the life that alone makes practical investigation safe and possible."

And towards the question of clairvoyance, too, his attitude was significantly sane, for he knew how extremely rare the genuine power was, and that what is commonly called clairvoyance is nothing more than a keen power of visualizing.

"It connotes a slightly increased sensibility, nothing more," he would say. "The true clairvoyant deplores his power, recognizing that it adds a new horror to life, and is in the nature of an affliction. And you will find this always to be the real test."

Thus it was that John Silence, this singularly developed doctor, was able to select his cases with a clear knowledge of the difference between mere hysterical delusion and the kind of psychical affliction that claimed his special powers. It was never necessary for him to resort to the cheap mysteries of divination; for, as I have heard him observe, after the solution of some peculiarly intricate problem —

"Systems of divination, from geomancy down to reading by tea-leaves, are merely so many methods of obscuring the outer vision, in order that the inner vision may become open. Once the method is mastered, no system is necessary at all."

And the words were significant of the methods of this remarkable man, the keynote of whose power lay, perhaps, more than anything else, in the knowledge, first, that thought can act at a distance, and, secondly, that thought is dynamic and can accomplish material results.

"Learn how to *think*," he would have expressed it, "and you have learned to tap power at its source."

To look at — he was now past forty — he was sparely built, with speaking brown eyes in which shone the light of knowledge and self-confidence, while at the same time they made one think of that wondrous gentleness seen most often in the eyes of animals. A close beard concealed the mouth without disguising the grim determination of lips and jaw, and the face somehow conveyed an impression of transparency, almost of light, so delicately were the features refined away. On the fine forehead was that indefinable touch of peace that comes from identifying the mind with what is permanent in the soul, and letting the impermanent slip by without power to wound or distress; while, from his manner, — so gentle, quiet, sympathetic, — few could have guessed the strength of purpose that burned within like a great flame.

"I think I should describe it as a psychical case," continued the Swedish lady, obviously trying to explain herself very intelligently, "and just the kind you like. I mean a case where the cause is hidden deep down in some spiritual distress, and — "

"But the symptoms first, please, my dear Svenska," he interrupted, with a strangely compelling seriousness of manner, "and your deductions afterwards."

She turned round sharply on the edge of her chair and looked him in the face, lowering her voice to prevent her emotion betraying itself too obviously.

"In my opinion there's only one symptom," she half whispered, as though telling something disagreeable — "fear — simply fear."

"Physical fear?"

"I think not; though how can I say? I think it's a horror in the psychical region. It's no ordinary delusion; the man is quite sane; but he lives in mortal terror of something — "

"I don't know what you mean by his 'psychical region,'" said the doctor, with a smile; "though I suppose you wish me to understand that his spiritual, and not his mental, processes are affected. Anyhow, try and tell me briefly and pointedly what you know about the man, his symptoms, his need for help, *my* peculiar help, that is, and all that seems vital in the case. I promise to listen devotedly."

"I am trying," she continued earnestly, "but must do so in my own words and trust to your intelligence to disentangle as I go along. He is a young author, and lives in a tiny house off Putney Heath somewhere. He writes humorous stories — quite a genre of his own: Pender — you must have heard the name — Felix Pender? Oh, the man had a great gift, and married on the strength of it; his future seemed assured. I say 'had,' for quite suddenly his talent utterly failed him. Worse, it became transformed into its opposite. He can no longer write a line in the old way that was bringing him success — "

Dr. Silence opened his eyes for a second and looked at her.

"He still writes, then? The force has not gone?" he asked briefly, and then closed his eyes again to listen.

"He works like a fury," she went on, "but produces nothing" — she hesitated a moment — "nothing that he can use or sell. His earnings have practically ceased, and he makes a precarious living by book-reviewing and odd jobs — very odd, some of them. Yet, I am certain his talent has not really deserted him finally, but is merely — "

Again Mrs. Sivendson hesitated for the appropriate word.

"In abeyance," he suggested, without opening his eyes.

"Obliterated," she went on, after a moment to weigh the word, "merely obliterated by something else — "

"By some *one* else?"

"I wish I knew. All I can say is that he is haunted, and temporarily his sense of humour is shrouded — gone — replaced by something dreadful that writes other things. Unless something competent is done, he will simply starve to death. Yet he is afraid to go to a doctor for fear of being pronounced insane; and, anyhow, a man can hardly ask a doctor to take a guinea to restore a vanished sense of humour, can he?"

"Has he tried any one at all — ?"

"Not doctors yet. He tried some clergymen and religious people; but they *know* so little and have so little intelligent sympathy. And most of them are so busy balancing on their own little pedestals — "

John Silence stopped her tirade with a gesture.

"And how is it that you know so much about him?" he asked gently.

"I know Mrs. Pender well — I knew her before she married him — "

"And is she a cause, perhaps?"

"Not in the least. She is devoted; a woman very well educated, though without being really intelligent, and with so little sense of humour herself that she always laughs at the wrong places. But she has nothing to do with the cause of his distress; and, indeed, has chiefly guessed it from observing him, rather than from what little he has told her. And he, you know, is a really lovable fellow, hard-working, patient — altogether worth saving."

Dr. Silence opened his eyes and went over to ring for tea. He did not know very much more about the case of the humorist than when he first sat down to listen; but he realized that no amount of words from his Swedish friend would help to reveal the real facts. A personal interview with the author himself could alone do that.

"All humorists are worth saving," he said with a smile, as she poured out tea. "We can't afford to lose a single one in these strenuous days. I will go and see your friend at the first opportunity."

She thanked him elaborately, effusively, with many words, and he, with much difficulty, kept the conversation thenceforward strictly to the teapot.

And, as a result of this conversation, and a little more he had gathered by means best known to himself and his secretary, he was whizzing in his motor-car one afternoon a few days later up the Putney Hill to have his first interview with Felix Pender, the humorous writer who was the victim of some mysterious malady in his "psychical region" that had obliterated his sense of the comic and threatened to wreck his life and destroy his talent. And his desire to help was probably of equal strength with his desire to know and to investigate.

The motor stopped with a deep purring sound, as though a great black panther lay concealed within its hood, and the doctor — the "psychic doctor," as he was sometimes called — stepped out through the gathering fog, and walked across the tiny garden that held a blackened fir tree and a stunted laurel shrubbery. The house was very small, and it was some time before any one answered the bell. Then, suddenly, a light appeared in the hall, and he saw a pretty little woman standing on the top step begging him to come in. She was dressed in grey, and the gaslight fell on a mass of deliberately brushed light hair. Stuffed, dusty birds, and a shabby array of African spears, hung on the wall behind her. A hat-rack, with a bronze plate full of very large cards, led his eye swiftly to a dark staircase beyond. Mrs. Pender had round eyes like a child's, and she greeted him with an effusiveness that barely concealed her emotion, yet strove to appear naturally cordial. Evidently she had been looking out for his arrival, and had outrun the servant girl. She was a little breathless.

"I hope you've not been kept waiting — I think it's *most* good of you to come — " she began, and then stopped sharp when she saw his face in the gaslight. There was something in Dr. Silence's look that did not encourage mere talk. He was in earnest now, if ever man was.

"Good evening, Mrs. Pender," he said, with a quiet smile that won confidence, yet deprecated unnecessary words, "the fog delayed me a little. I am glad to see you."

They went into a dingy sitting-room at the back of the house, neatly furnished but depressing. Books stood in a row upon the mantelpiece. The fire had evidently just been lit. It smoked in great puffs into the room.

"Mrs. Sivendson said she thought you might be able to come," ventured the little woman again, looking up engagingly into his face and betraying anxiety and eagerness in every gesture. "But I hardly dared to believe it. I think it is really too good of you. My husband's case is so peculiar that — well, you know, I am quite sure any *ordinary* doctor would say at once the asylum — "

"Isn't he in, then?" asked Dr. Silence gently.

"In the asylum?" she gasped. "Oh dear, no — not yet!"

"In the house, I meant," he laughed.

She gave a great sigh.

"He'll be back any minute now," she replied, obviously relieved to see him laugh; "but the fact is, we didn't expect you so early — I mean, my husband hardly thought you would come at all."

"I am always delighted to come — when I am really wanted, and can be of help," he said quickly; "and, perhaps, it's all for the best that your husband is out, for now that we are alone you can tell me something about his difficulties. So far, you know, I have heard very little."

Her voice trembled as she thanked him, and when he came and took a chair close beside her she actually had difficulty in finding words with which to begin.

"In the first place," she began timidly, and then continuing with a nervous incoherent rush of words, "he will be simply delighted that you've really come, because he said you were the only person he would consent to see at all — the only doctor, I mean. But, of course, he doesn't know how frightened I am, or how much I have noticed. He pretends with me that it's just a nervous breakdown, and I'm sure he doesn't realize all the odd things I've noticed him doing. But the main thing, I suppose — "

"Yes, the main thing, Mrs. Pender," he said encouragingly, noticing her hesitation.

" — is that he thinks we are not alone in the house. That's the chief thing."

"Tell me more facts — just facts."

"It began last summer when I came back from Ireland; he had been here alone for six weeks, and I thought him looking tired and queer — ragged and scattered about the face, if you know what I mean, and his manner worn out. He said he had been writing hard, but his inspiration had somehow failed him, and he was dissatisfied with his work. His sense of humour was leaving him, or changing into something else, he said. There was something in the house, he declared, that" — she emphasized the words — "prevented his feeling funny."

"Something in the house that prevented his feeling funny," repeated the doctor. "Ah, now we're getting to the heart of it!"

"Yes," she resumed vaguely, "that's what he kept saying."

"And what was it he *did* that you thought strange?" he asked sympathetically. "Be brief, or he may be here before you finish."

"Very small things, but significant it seemed to me. He changed his workroom from the library, as we call it, to the sitting-room. He said all his characters became wrong and terrible in the library; they altered, so that he felt like writing tragedies — vile, debased tragedies, the tragedies of broken souls. But now he says the same of the smoking-room, and he's gone back to the library."

"Ah!"

"You see, there's so little I can tell you," she went on, with increasing speed and countless gestures. "I mean it's only very small things he does and says that are queer. What frightens me is that he assumes there is some one else in the house all the time — some one I never see. He does not actually say so, but on the stairs I've seen him standing aside to let some one pass; I've seen him open a door to let some one in or out; and often in our bedroom he puts chairs about as though for some one else to sit in. Oh — oh yes, and once or twice," she cried — "once or twice — "

She paused, and looked about her with a startled air.

"Yes?"

"Once or twice," she resumed hurriedly, as though she heard a sound that alarmed her, "I've heard him running — coming in and out of the rooms breathless as if something were after him — "

The door opened while she was still speaking, cutting her words off in the middle, and a man came into the room. He was dark and clean-shaven sallow rather, with the eyes of imagination, and dark hair growing scantily about the temples. He was dressed in a shabby tweed suit, and wore an untidy flannel collar at the neck. The dominant expression of his face was startled — hunted; an expression that might any moment leap into the dreadful stare of terror and announce a total loss of self-control.

The moment he saw his visitor a smile spread over his worn features, and he advanced to shake hands.

"I hoped you would come; Mrs. Sivendson said you might be able to find time," he said simply. His voice was thin and reedy. "I am very glad to see you, Dr. Silence. It is 'Doctor,' is it not?"

"Well, I am entitled to the description," laughed the other, "but I rarely get it. You know, I do not practice as a regular thing; that is, I only take cases that specially interest me, or — "

He did not finish the sentence, for the men exchanged a glance of sympathy that rendered it unnecessary.

"I have heard of your great kindness."

"It's my hobby," said the other quickly, "and my privilege."

"I trust you will still think so when you have heard what I have to tell you," continued the author, a little wearily. He led the way across the hall into the little smoking-room where they could talk freely and undisturbed.

In the smoking-room, the door shut and privacy about them, Pender's attitude changed somewhat, and his manner became very grave. The doctor sat opposite, where he could watch his face. Already, he saw, it looked more haggard. Evidently it cost him much to refer to his trouble at all.

"What I have is, in my belief, a profound spiritual affliction," he began quite bluntly, looking straight into the other's eyes.

"I saw that at once," Dr. Silence said.

"Yes, you saw that, of course; my atmosphere must convey that much to any one with psychic perceptions. Besides which, I feel sure from all I have heard, that you are really a soul-doctor, are you not, more than a healer merely of the body?"

"You think of me too highly," returned the other; "though I prefer cases, as you know, in which the spirit is disturbed first, the body afterwards."

"I understand, yes. Well, I have experienced a curious disturbance in — *not* in my physical region primarily. I mean my nerves are all right, and my body is all right. I have no delusions exactly, but my spirit is tortured by a calamitous fear which first came upon me in a strange manner."

John Silence leaned forward a moment and took the speaker's hand and held it in his own for a few brief seconds,

closing his eyes as he did so. He was not feeling his pulse, or doing any of the things that doctors ordinarily do; he was merely
absorbing into himself the main note of the man's mental condition, so as to get completely his own point of view, and thus be
able to treat his case with true sympathy. A very close observer
might perhaps have noticed that a slight tremor ran through his
frame after he had held the hand for a few seconds.

"Tell me quite frankly, Mr. Pender," he said soothingly, releasing the hand, and with deep attention in his manner, "tell me
all the steps that led to the beginning of this invasion. I mean tell
me what the particular drug was, and why you took it, and how
it affected you — "

"Then you know it began with a drug!" cried the author,
with undisguised astonishment.

"I only know from what I observe in you, and in its effect
upon myself. You are in a surprising psychical condition. Certain
portions of your atmosphere are vibrating at a far greater rate
than others. This is the effect of a drug, but of no ordinary drug.
Allow me to finish, please. If the higher rate of vibration spreads
all over, you will become, of course, permanently cognisant of a
much larger world than the one you know normally. If, on the
other hand, the rapid portion sinks back to the usual rate, you
will lose these occasional increased perceptions you now have."

"You amaze me!" exclaimed the author; "for your words exactly describe what I have been feeling — "

"I mention this only in passing, and to give you confidence
before you approach the account of your real affliction," continued the doctor. "All perception, as you know, is the result of vibrations; and clairvoyance simply means becoming sensitive to
an increased scale of vibrations. The awakening of the inner
senses we hear so much about means no more than that. Your
partial clairvoyance is easily explained. The only thing that puz-
zles me is how you managed to procure the drug, for it is not
easy to get in pure form, and no adulterated tincture could have
given you the terrific impetus I see you have acquired. But, please
proceed now and tell me your story in your own way."

"This *Cannabis indica*," the author went on, "came into my possession last autumn while my wife was away. I need not explain how I got it, for that has no importance; but it was the genuine fluid extract, and I could not resist the temptation to make an experiment. One of its effects, as you know, is to induce torrential laughter — "

"Yes; sometimes."

" — I am a writer of humorous tales, and I wished to increase my own sense of laughter — to see the ludicrous from an abnormal point of view. I wished to study it a bit, if possible, and — "

"Tell me!"

"I took an experimental dose. I starved for six hours to hasten the effect, locked myself into this room, and gave orders not to be disturbed. Then I swallowed the stuff and waited."

"And the effect?"

"I waited one hour, two, three, four, five hours. Nothing happened. No laughter came, but only a great weariness instead. Nothing in the room or in my thoughts came within a hundred miles of a humorous aspect."

"Always a most uncertain drug," interrupted the doctor. "We make a very small use of it on that account."

"At two o'clock in the morning I felt so hungry and tired that I decided to give up the experiment and wait no longer. I drank some milk and went upstairs to bed. I felt flat and disappointed. I fell asleep at once and must have slept for about an hour, when I awoke suddenly with a great noise in my ears. It was the noise of my own laughter! I was simply shaking with merriment. At first I was bewildered and thought I had been laughing in dreams, but a moment later I remembered the drug, and was delighted to think that after all I had got an effect. It had been working all along, only I had miscalculated the time. The only unpleasant thing *then* was an odd feeling that I had not waked naturally, but had been wakened by some one else — deliberately. This came to me as a certainty in the middle of my noisy laughter and distressed me."

"Any impression who it could have been?" asked the doctor, now listening with close attention to every word, very much on the alert.

Pender hesitated and tried to smile. He brushed his hair from his forehead with a nervous gesture.

"You must tell me all your impressions, even your fancies; they are quite as important as your certainties."

"I had a vague idea that it was some one connected with my forgotten dream, some one who had been at me in my sleep, some one of great strength and great ability — or great force — quite an unusual personality — and, I was certain, too — a woman."

"A good woman?" asked John Silence quietly.

Pender started a little at the question and his sallow face flushed; it seemed to surprise him. But he shook his head quickly with an indefinable look of horror.

"Evil," he answered briefly, "appallingly evil, and yet mingled with the sheer wickedness of it was also a certain perverseness — the perversity of the unbalanced mind."

He hesitated a moment and looked up sharply at his interlocutor. A shade of suspicion showed itself in his eyes.

"No," laughed the doctor, "you need not fear that I'm merely humouring you, or think you mad. Far from it. Your story interests me exceedingly and you furnish me unconsciously with a number of clues as you tell it. You see, I possess some knowledge of my own as to these psychic byways."

"I was shaking with such violent laughter," continued the narrator, reassured in a moment, "though with no clear idea what was amusing me, that I had the greatest difficulty in getting up for the matches, and was afraid I should frighten the servants overhead with my explosions. When the gas was lit I found the room empty, of course, and the door locked as usual. Then I half dressed and went out on to the landing, my hilarity better under control, and proceeded to go downstairs. I wished to record my sensations. I stuffed a handkerchief into my mouth so as not to scream aloud and communicate my hysterics to the entire household."

"And the presence of this — this — ?"

"It was hanging about me all the time," said Pender, "but for the moment it seemed to have withdrawn. Probably, too, my laughter killed all other emotions."

"And how long did you take getting downstairs?"

"I was just coming to that. I see you know all my 'symptoms' in advance, as it were; for, of course, I thought I should never get to the bottom. Each step seemed to take five minutes, and crossing the narrow hall at the foot of the stairs — well, I could have sworn it was half an hour's journey had not my watch certified that it was a few seconds. Yet I walked fast and tried to push on. It was no good. I walked apparently without advancing, and at that rate it would have taken me a week to get down Putney Hill."

"An experimental dose radically alters the scale of time and space sometimes — "

"But, when at last I got into my study and lit the gas, the change came horridly, and sudden as a flash of lightning. It was like a douche of icy water, and in the middle of this storm of laughter — "

"Yes; what?" asked the doctor, leaning forward and peering into his eyes.

" — I was overwhelmed with terror," said Pender, lowering his reedy voice at the mere recollection of it.

He paused a moment and mopped his forehead. The scared, hunted look in his eyes now dominated the whole face. Yet, all the time, the corners of his mouth hinted of possible laughter as though the recollection of that merriment still amused him. The combination of fear and laughter in his face was very curious, and lent great conviction to his story; it also lent a bizarre expression of horror to his gestures.

"Terror, was it?" repeated the doctor soothingly.

"Yes, terror; for, though the Thing that woke me seemed to have gone, the memory of it still frightened me, and I collapsed into a chair. Then I locked the door and tried to reason with myself, but the drug made my movements so prolonged that it took me five minutes to reach the door, and another five to get back to the chair again. The laughter, too, kept bubbling up inside me — great wholesome laughter that shook me like gusts of wind — so that even my terror almost made me laugh. Oh, but I may tell you, Dr. Silence, it was altogether vile, that mixture of fear and laughter, altogether vile!

"Then, all at once, the things in the room again presented their funny side to me and set me off laughing more furiously than ever. The bookcase was ludicrous, the arm-chair a perfect clown, the way the clock looked at me on the mantelpiece too comic for words; the arrangement of papers and inkstand on the desk tickled me till I roared and shook and held my sides and the tears streamed down my cheeks. And that footstool! Oh, that absurd footstool!"

He lay back in his chair, laughing to himself and holding up his hands at the thought of it, and at the sight of him Dr. Silence laughed too.

"Go on, please," he said, "I quite understand. I know something myself of the hashish laughter."

The author pulled himself together and resumed, his face growing quickly grave again.

"So, you see, side by side with this extravagant, apparently causeless merriment, there was also an extravagant, apparently causeless, terror. The drug produced the laughter, I knew; but what brought in the terror I could not imagine. Everywhere behind the fun lay the fear. It was terror masked by cap and bells; and I became the playground for two opposing emotions, armed and fighting to the death. Gradually, then, the impression grew in me that this fear was caused by the invasion — so you called it just now — of the 'person' who had wakened me; she was utterly evil; inimical to my soul, or at least to all in me that wished for good. There I stood, sweating and trembling, laughing at everything in the room, yet all the while with this white terror mastering my heart. And this creature was putting — putting her — "

He hesitated again, using his handkerchief freely.

"Putting what?"

" — putting ideas into my mind," he went on, glancing nervously about the room. "Actually tapping my thought-stream so as to switch off the usual current and inject her own. How mad that sounds! I know it, but it's true. It's the only way I can express it. Moreover, while the operation terrified me, the skill with which it was accomplished filled me afresh with laughter at the clumsiness of men by comparison. Our ignorant, bungling methods of teaching the minds of others, of inculcating ideas, and so on, overwhelmed me with laughter when I understood this superior and diabolical method. Yet my laughter seemed hollow and ghastly, and ideas of evil and tragedy trod close upon the heels of the comic. Oh, doctor, I tell you again, it was unnerving!"

John Silence sat with his head thrust forward to catch every word of the story which the other continued to pour out in nervous, jerky sentences and lowered voice.

"You *saw* nothing — no one — all this time?" he asked.

"Not with my eyes. There was no visual hallucination. But in my mind there began to grow the vivid picture of a woman — large, dark-skinned, with white teeth and masculine features, and one eye — the left — so drooping as to appear almost closed. Oh, such a face — !"

"A face you would recognize again?"

Pender laughed dreadfully.

"I wish I could forget it," he whispered, "I only wish I could forget it!" Then he sat forward in his chair suddenly, and grasped the doctor's hand with an emotional gesture.

"I *must* tell you how grateful I am for your patience and sympathy," he cried, with a tremor in his voice, "and — that you do not think me mad. I have told no one else a quarter of all this, and the mere freedom of speech — the relief of sharing my affliction with another — has helped me already more than I can possibly say."

Dr. Silence pressed his hand and looked steadily into the frightened eyes. His voice was very gentle when he replied.

"Your case, you know, is very singular, but of absorbing interest to me," he said, "for it threatens, not your physical existence, but the temple of your psychical existence — the inner life. Your mind would not be permanently affected here and now, in this world; but in the existence after the body is left behind, you might wake up with your spirit so twisted, so distorted, so befouled, that you would be *spiritually insane* — a far more radical condition than merely being insane here."

There came a strange hush over the room, and between the two men sitting there facing one another.

"Do you really mean — Good Lord!" stammered the author as soon as he could find his tongue.

"What I mean in detail will keep till a little later, and I need only say now that I should not have spoken in this way unless I were quite positive of being able to help you. Oh, there's no doubt as to that, believe me. In the first place, I am very familiar with the workings of this extraordinary drug, this drug which has had the chance effect of opening you up to the forces of another region; and, in the second, I have a firm belief in the reality of super-sensuous occurrences as well as considerable knowledge of psychic processes acquired by long and painful experiment. The rest is, or should be, merely sympathetic treatment and practical application. The hashish has partially opened another world to you by increasing your rate of psychical vibration, and thus rendering you abnormally sensitive. Ancient forces attached to this house have attacked you. For the moment I am only puzzled as to their precise nature; for were they of an ordinary character, I should myself be psychic enough to feel them. Yet I am conscious of feeling nothing as yet. But now, please continue, Mr. Pender, and tell me the rest of your wonderful story; and when you have finished, I will talk about the means of cure."

Pender shifted his chair a little closer to the friendly doctor and then went on in the same nervous voice with his narrative.

"After making some notes of my impressions I finally got upstairs again to bed. It was four o'clock in the morning. I laughed all the way up — at the grotesque banisters, the droll physiognomy of the staircase window, the burlesque grouping of the furniture, and the memory of that outrageous footstool in the room below; but nothing more happened to alarm or disturb me, and I woke late in the morning after a dreamless sleep, none the worse for my experiment except for a slight headache and a coldness of the extremities due to lowered circulation."

"Fear gone, too?" asked the doctor.

"I seemed to have forgotten it, or at least ascribed it to mere nervousness. Its reality had gone, anyhow for the time, and all that day I wrote and wrote and wrote. My sense of laughter seemed wonderfully quickened and my characters acted without effort out of the heart of true humour. I was exceedingly pleased with this result of my experiment. But when the stenographer had taken her departure and I came to read over the pages she had typed out, I recalled her sudden glances of surprise and the odd way she had looked up at me while I was dictating. I was amazed at what I read and could hardly believe I had uttered it."

"And why?"

"It was so distorted. The words, indeed, were mine so far as I could remember, but the meanings seemed strange. It frightened me. The sense was so altered. At the very places where my characters were intended to tickle the ribs, only curious emotions of sinister amusement resulted. Dreadful innuendoes had managed to creep into the phrases. There was laughter of a kind, but it was bizarre, horrible, distressing; and my attempt at analysis only increased my dismay. The story, as it read then, made me shudder, for by virtue of these slight changes it had come somehow to hold the soul of horror, of horror disguised as merriment. The framework of humour was there, if you understand me, but the characters had turned sinister, and their laughter was evil."

"Can you show me this writing?"

The author shook his head.

"I destroyed it," he whispered. "But, in the end, though of course much perturbed about it, I persuaded myself that it was due to some after-effect of the drug, a sort of reaction that gave a twist to my mind and made me read macabre interpretations into words and situations that did not properly hold them."

"And, meanwhile, did the presence of this person leave you?"

"No; that stayed more or less. When my mind was actively employed I forgot it, but when idle, dreaming, or doing nothing in particular, there she was beside me, influencing my mind horribly — "

"In what way, precisely?" interrupted the doctor.

"Evil, scheming thoughts came to me, visions of crime, hateful pictures of wickedness, and the kind of bad imagination that so far has been foreign, indeed impossible, to my normal nature — "

"The pressure of the Dark Powers upon the personality," murmured the doctor, making a quick note.

"Eh? I didn't quite catch — "

"Pray, go on. I am merely making notes; you shall know their purport fully later."

"Even when my wife returned I was still aware of this Presence in the house; it associated itself with my inner personality in most intimate fashion; and outwardly I always felt oddly constrained to be polite and respectful towards it — to open doors, provide chairs and hold myself carefully deferential when it was about. It became very compelling at last, and, if I failed in any little particular, I seemed to know that it pursued me about the house, from one room to another, haunting my very soul in its inmost abode. It certainly came before my wife so far as my attentions were concerned.

"But, let me first finish the story of my experimental dose, for I took it again the third night, and underwent a very similar experience, delayed like the first in coming, and then carrying me off my feet when it did come with a rush of this false demon-laughter. This time, however, there was a reversal of the changed scale of space and time; it shortened instead of lengthened, so that I dressed and got downstairs in about twenty seconds, and the couple of hours I stayed and worked in the study passed literally like a period of ten minutes."

"That is often true of an overdose," interjected the doctor, "and you may go a mile in a few minutes, or a few yards in a quarter of an hour. It is quite incomprehensible to those who have never experienced it, and is a curious proof that time and space are merely forms of thought."

"This time," Pender went on, talking more and more rapidly in his excitement, "another extraordinary effect came to me, and I experienced a curious changing of the senses, so that I perceived external things through one large main sense-channel instead of through the five divisions known as sight, smell, touch, and so forth. You will, I know, understand me when I tell you that I *heard* sights and *saw* sounds. No language can make this comprehensible, of course, and I can only say, for instance, that the striking of the clock I saw as a visible picture in the air before me. I saw the sounds of the tinkling bell. And in precisely the same way I heard the colours in the room, especially the colours of those books in the shelf behind you. Those red bindings I heard in deep sounds, and the yellow covers of the French bindings next to them made a shrill, piercing note not unlike the chattering of starlings. That brown bookcase muttered, and those green curtains opposite kept up a constant sort of rippling sound like the lower notes of a woodhorn. But I only was conscious of these sounds when I looked steadily at the different objects, and thought about them. The room, you understand, was not full of a chorus of notes; but when I concentrated my mind upon a colour,

I heard, as well as saw, it."

"That is a known, though rarely-obtained, effect of *Cannabis indica*," observed the doctor. "And it provoked laughter again, did it?"

"Only the muttering of the cupboard-bookcase made me laugh. It was so like a great animal trying to get itself noticed, and made me think of a performing bear — which is full of a kind of pathetic humour, you know. But this mingling of the senses produced no confusion in my brain. On the contrary, I was unusually clear-headed and experienced an intensification of consciousness, and felt marvellously alive and keen-minded.

"Moreover, when I took up a pencil in obedience to an impulse to sketch — a talent not normally mine — I found that I could draw nothing but heads, nothing, in fact, but one head — always the same — the head of a dark-skinned woman, with huge and terrible features and a very drooping left eye; and so well drawn, too, that I was amazed, as you may imagine — "

"And the expression of the face — ?"

Pender hesitated a moment for words, casting about with his hands in the air and hunching his shoulders. A perceptible shudder ran over him.

"What I can only describe as — *blackness*," he replied in a low tone; "the face of a dark and evil soul."

"You destroyed that, too?" queried the doctor sharply.

"No; I have kept the drawings," he said, with a laugh, and rose to get them from a drawer in the writing-desk behind him.

"Here is all that remains of the pictures, you see," he added, pushing a number of loose sheets under the doctor's eyes; "nothing but a few scrawly lines. That's all I found the next morning. I had really drawn no heads at all — nothing but those lines and blots and wriggles. The pictures were entirely subjective, and existed only in my mind which constructed them out of a few wild strokes of the pen. Like the altered scale of space and time it was a complete delusion. These all passed, of course, with the passing of the drug's effects. But the other thing did not pass. I mean, the presence of that Dark Soul remained with me. It is here still. It is real. I don't know how I can escape from it."

"It is attached to the house, not to you personally. You must leave the house."

"Yes. Only I cannot afford to leave the house, for my work is my sole means of support, and — well, you see, since this change I cannot even write. They are horrible, these mirthless tales I now write, with their mockery of laughter, their diabolical suggestion. Horrible! I shall go mad if this continues."

He screwed his face up and looked about the room as though he expected to see some haunting shape.

"The influence in this house, induced by my experiment, has killed in a flash, in a sudden stroke, the sources of my humour, and, though I still go on writing funny tales — I have a certain name, you know — my inspiration has dried up, and much of what I write I have to burn — yes, doctor, to burn, before any one sees it."

"As utterly alien to your own mind and personality?"

"Utterly! As though some one else had written it — "

"Ah!"

"And shocking!" He passed his hand over his eyes a moment and let the breath escape softly through his teeth. "Yet most damnably clever in the consummate way the vile suggestions are insinuated under cover of a kind of high drollery. My stenographer left me, of course — and I've been afraid to take another — "

John Silence got up and began to walk about the room leisurely without speaking; he appeared to be examining the pictures on the wall and reading the names of the books lying about. Presently he paused on the hearthrug, with his back to the fire, and turned to look his patient quietly in the eyes. Pender's face was grey and drawn; the hunted expression dominated it; the long recital had told upon him.

"Thank you, Mr. Pender," he said, a curious glow showing about his fine, quiet face, "thank you for the sincerity and frankness of your account. But I think now there is nothing further I need ask you." He indulged in a long scrutiny of the author's haggard features, drawing purposely the man's eyes to his own and then meeting them with a look of power and confidence calculated to inspire even the feeblest soul with courage. "And, to begin with," he added, smiling pleasantly, "let me assure you without delay that you need have no alarm, for you are no more insane or deluded than I myself am — "

Pender heaved a deep sigh and tried to return the smile.

" — and this is simply a case, so far as I can judge at present, of a very singular psychical invasion, and a very sinister one, too, if you perhaps understand what I mean — "

"It's an odd expression; you used it before, you know," said the author wearily, yet eagerly listening to every word of the diagnosis, and deeply touched by the intelligent sympathy which did not at once indicate the lunatic asylum.

"Possibly," returned the other, "and an odd affliction too, you'll allow, yet one not unknown to the nations of antiquity, nor to those moderns, perhaps, who recognize the freedom of action under certain pathogenic conditions between this world and another."

"And you think," asked Pender hastily, "that it is all primarily due to the *Cannabis*? There is nothing radically amiss with myself — nothing incurable, or — ?"

"Due entirely to the overdose," Dr. Silence replied emphatically, "to the drug's direct action upon your psychical being. It rendered you ultra-sensitive and made you respond to an increased rate of vibration. And, let me tell you, Mr. Pender, that your experiment might have had results far more dire. It has brought you into touch with a somewhat singular class of Invisible, but of one, I think, chiefly human in character. You might, however, just as easily have been drawn out of human range altogether, and the results of such a contingency would have been exceedingly terrible. Indeed, you would not now be here to tell the tale. I need not alarm you on that score, but mention it as a warning you will not misunderstand or underrate after what you have been through.

"You look puzzled. You do not quite gather what I am driving at; and it is not to be expected that you should, for you, I suppose, are the nominal Christian with the nominal Christian's lofty standard of ethics, and his utter ignorance of spiritual possibilities. Beyond a somewhat childish understanding of 'spiritual wickedness in high places,' you probably have no conception of what is possible once you break down the slender gulf that is mercifully fixed between you and that Outer World. But my studies and training have taken me far outside these orthodox trips, and I have made experiments that I could scarcely speak to you about in language that would be intelligible to you."

He paused a moment to note the breathless interest of Pender's face and manner. Every word he uttered was calculated; he knew exactly the value and effect of the emotions he desired to waken in the heart of the afflicted being before him.

"And from certain knowledge I have gained through various experiences," he continued calmly, "I can diagnose your case as I said before to be one of psychical invasion."

"And the nature of this — er — invasion?" stammered the bewildered writer of humorous tales.

"There is no reason why I should not say at once that I do not yet quite know," replied Dr. Silence. "I may first have to make one or two experiments — "

"On me?" gasped Pender, catching his breath.

"Not exactly," the doctor said, with a grave smile, "but with your assistance, perhaps. I shall want to test the conditions of the house — to ascertain, if possible, the character of the forces, of this strange personality that has been haunting you — "

"At present you have no idea exactly who — what — why — " asked the other in a wild flurry of interest, dread and amazement.

"I have a very good idea, but no proof rather," returned the doctor. "The effects of the drug in altering the scale of time and space, and merging the senses have nothing primarily to do with the invasion. They come to any one who is fool enough to take an experimental dose. It is the other features of your case that are unusual. You see, you are now in touch with certain violent emotions, desires, purposes, still active in this house, that were produced in the past by some powerful and evil personality that lived here. How long ago, or why they still persist so forcibly, I cannot positively say. But I should judge that they are merely forces acting automatically with the momentum of their terrific original impetus."

"Not directed by a living being, a conscious will, you mean?"

"Possibly not — but none the less dangerous on that account, and more difficult to deal with. I cannot explain to you in a few minutes the nature of such things, for you have not made the studies that would enable you to follow me; but I have reason to believe that on the dissolution at death of a human being, its forces may still persist and continue to act in a blind, unconscious fashion. As a rule they speedily dissipate themselves, but in the case of a very powerful personality they may last a long time. And, in some cases — of which I incline to think this is one — these forces may coalesce with certain non-human entities who thus continue their life indefinitely and increase their strength to an unbelievable degree. If the original personality was evil, the beings attracted to the left-over forces will also be evil. In this case, I think there has been an unusual and dreadful aggrandizement of the thoughts and purposes left behind long ago by a woman of consummate wickedness and great personal power of character and intellect. Now, do you begin to see what I am driving at a little?"

Pender stared fixedly at his companion, plain horror showing in his eyes. But he found nothing to say, and the doctor continued —

"In your case, predisposed by the action of the drug, you

have experienced the rush of these forces in undiluted strength. They wholly obliterate in you the sense of humour, fancy, imagination, — all that makes for cheerfulness and hope. They seek, though perhaps automatically only, to oust your own thoughts and establish themselves in their place. You are the victim of a psychical invasion. At the same time, you have become clairvoyant in the true sense. You are also a clairvoyant victim."

Pender mopped his face and sighed. He left his chair and went over to the fireplace to warm himself.

"You must think me a quack to talk like this, or a madman," laughed Dr. Silence. "But never mind that. I have come to help you, and I can help you if you will do what I tell you. It is very simple: you must leave this house at once. Oh, never mind the difficulties; we will deal with those together. I can place another house at your disposal, or I would take the lease here off your hands, and later have it pulled down. Your case interests me greatly, and I mean to see you through, so you have no anxiety, and can drop back into your old groove of work tomorrow! The drug has provided you, and therefore me, with a short-cut to a very interesting experience. I am grateful to you."

The author poked the fire vigorously, emotion rising in him like a tide. He glanced towards the door nervously.

"There is no need to alarm your wife or to tell her the details of our conversation," pursued the other quietly. "Let her know that you will soon be in possession again of your sense of humour and your health, and explain that I am lending you another house for six months. Meanwhile I may have the right to use this house for a night or two for my experiment. Is that understood between us?"

"I can only thank you from the bottom of my heart," stammered Pender, unable to find words to express his gratitude.

Then he hesitated for a moment, searching the doctor's face anxiously.

"And your experiment with the house?" he said at length.

"Of the simplest character, my dear Mr. Pender. Although I am myself an artificially trained psychic, and consequently aware of the presence of discarnate entities as a rule, I have so far felt nothing here at all. This makes me sure that the forces acting here are of an unusual description. What I propose to do is to make an experiment with a view of drawing out this evil, coaxing it from its lair, so to speak, in order that it may *exhaust itself through me* and become dissipated for ever. I have already been inoculated," he added; "I consider myself to be immune."

"Heavens above!" gasped the author, collapsing on to a chair.

"Hell beneath! might be a more appropriate exclamation," the doctor laughed. "But, seriously, Mr. Pender, that is what I propose to do — with your permission."

"Of course, of course," cried the other, "you have my permission and my best wishes for success. I can see no possible objection, but — "

"But what?"

"I pray to Heaven you will not undertake this experiment alone, will you?"

"Oh dear, no; not alone."

"You will take a companion with good nerves, and reliable in case of disaster, won't you?"

"I shall bring two companions," the doctor said.

"Ah, that's better. I feel easier. I am sure you must have among your acquaintances men who — "

"I shall not think of bringing men, Mr. Pender."

The other looked up sharply.

"No, or women either; or children."

"I don't understand. Who will you bring, then?"

"Animals," explained the doctor, unable to prevent a smile at his companion's expression of surprise — "two animals, a cat and a dog."

49

Pender stared as if his eyes would drop out upon the floor, and then led the way without another word into the adjoining room where his wife was awaiting them for tea.

II

A few days later the humorist and his wife, with minds greatly relieved, moved into a small furnished house placed at their free disposal in another part of London; and John Silence, intent upon his approaching experiment, made ready to spend a night in the empty house on the top of Putney Hill. Only two rooms were prepared for occupation: the study on the ground floor and the bedroom immediately above it; all other doors were to be locked, and no servant was to be left in the house. The motor had orders to call for him at nine o'clock the following morning.

And, meanwhile, his secretary had instructions to look up the past history and associations of the place, and learn everything he could concerning the character of former occupants, recent or remote.

The animals, by whose sensitiveness he intended to test any unusual conditions in the atmosphere of the building, Dr. Silence selected with care and judgment. He believed (and had already made curious experiments to prove it) that animals were more often, and more truly, clairvoyant than human beings. Many of them, he felt convinced, possessed powers of perception far superior to that mere keenness of the senses common to all dwellers in the wilds where the senses grow specially alert; they had what he termed "animal clairvoyance," and from his experiments with horses, dogs, cats, and even birds, he had drawn certain deductions, which, however, need not be referred to in detail here.

Cats, in particular, he believed, were almost continuously conscious of a larger field of vision, too detailed even for a photographic camera, and quite beyond the reach of normal human organs. He had, further, observed that while dogs were usually terrified in the presence of such phenomena, cats on the other hand were soothed and satisfied. They welcomed manifestations as something belonging peculiarly to their own region.

He selected his animals, therefore, with wisdom so that they might afford a differing test, each in its own way, and that one should not merely communicate its own excitement to the other. He took a dog and a cat.

The cat he chose, now full grown, had lived with him since kittenhood, a kittenhood of perplexing sweetness and audacious mischief. Wayward it was and fanciful, ever playing its own mysterious games in the corners of the room, jumping at invisible nothings, leaping sideways into the air and falling with tiny mocassined feet on to another part of the carpet, yet with an air of dignified earnestness which showed that the performance was necessary to its own well-being, and not done merely to impress a stupid human audience. In the middle of elaborate washing it would look up, startled, as though to stare at the approach of some Invisible, cocking its little head sideways and putting out a velvet pad to inspect cautiously. Then it would get absent-minded, and stare with equal intentness in another direction (just to confuse the onlookers), and suddenly go on furiously washing its body again, but in quite a new place. Except for a white patch on its breast it was coal black. And its name was — Smoke.

"Smoke" described its temperament as well as its appearance. Its movements, its individuality, its posing as a little furry mass of concealed mysteries, its elfin-like elusiveness, all combined to justify its name; and a subtle painter might have pictured it as a wisp of floating smoke, the fire below betraying itself at two points only — the glowing eyes.

All its forces ran to intelligence — secret intelligence, wordless, incalculable intuition of the Cat. It was, indeed, *the* cat for the business in hand.

The selection of the dog was not so simple, for the doctor owned many; but after much deliberation he chose a collie, called Flame from his yellow coat. True, it was a trifle old, and stiff in the joints, and even beginning to grow deaf, but, on the other hand, it was a very particular friend of Smoke's, and had fathered it from kittenhood upwards so that a subtle understanding existed between them. It was this that turned the balance in its favour, this and its courage. Moreover, though good-tempered, it was a terrible fighter, and its anger when provoked by a righteous cause was a fury of fire, and irresistible.

It had come to him quite young, straight from the shepherd, with the air of the hills yet in its nostrils, and was then little more than skin and bones and teeth. For a collie it was sturdily built, its nose blunter than most, its yellow hair stiff rather than silky, and it had full eyes, unlike the slit eyes of its breed. Only its master could touch it, for it ignored strangers, and despised their pattings — when any dared to pat it. There was something patriarchal about the old beast. He was in earnest, and went through life with tremendous energy and big things in view, as though he had the reputation of his whole race to uphold. And to watch him fighting against odds was to understand why he was terrible.

In his relations with Smoke he was always absurdly gentle; also he was fatherly; and at the same time betrayed a certain diffidence or shyness. He recognized that Smoke called for strong yet respectful management. The cat's circuitous methods puzzled him, and his elaborate pretences perhaps shocked the dog's liking for direct, undisguised action. Yet, while he failed to comprehend these tortuous feline mysteries, he was never contemptuous or condescending; and he presided over the safety of his furry black friend somewhat as a father, loving but intuitive, might superintend the vagaries of a wayward and talented child. And, in return, Smoke rewarded him with exhibitions of fascinating and audacious mischief.

And these brief descriptions of their characters are necessary for the proper understanding of what subsequently took place.

With Smoke sleeping in the folds of his fur coat, and the collie lying watchful on the seat opposite, John Silence went down in his motor after dinner on the night of November 15th.

And the fog was so dense that they were obliged to travel at quarter speed the entire way.

It was after ten o'clock when he dismissed the motor and entered the dingy little house with the latchkey provided by Pender. He found the hall gas turned low, and a fire in the study. Books and food had also been placed ready by the servant according to instructions. Coils of fog rushed in after him through the opened door and filled the hall and passage with its cold discomfort.

The first thing Dr. Silence did was to lock up Smoke in the study with a saucer of milk before the fire, and then make a search of the house with Flame. The dog ran cheerfully behind him all the way while he tried the doors of the other rooms to make sure they were locked. He nosed about into corners and made little excursions on his own account. His manner was expectant. He knew there must be something unusual about the proceeding, because it was contrary to the habits of his whole life not to be asleep at this hour on the mat in front of the fire. He kept looking up into his master's face, as door after door was tried, with an expression of intelligent sympathy, but at the same time a certain air of disapproval. Yet everything his master did was good in his eyes, and he betrayed as little impatience as possible with all this unnecessary journeying to and fro. If the doctor was pleased to play this sort of game at such an hour of the night, it was surely not for him to object. So he played it too; and was very busy and earnest about it into the bargain.

After an uneventful search they came down again to the study, and here Dr. Silence discovered Smoke washing his face calmly in front of the fire. The saucer of milk was licked dry and clean; the preliminary examination that cats always make in new surroundings had evidently been satisfactorily concluded. He drew an arm-chair up to the fire, stirred the coals into a blaze, arranged the table and lamp to his satisfaction for reading, and then prepared surreptitiously to watch the animals. He wished to observe them carefully without their being aware of it.

Now, in spite of their respective ages, it was the regular custom of these two to play together every night before sleep. Smoke always made the advances, beginning with grave impudence to pat the dog's tail, and Flame played cumbrously, with condescension. It was his duty, rather than pleasure; he was glad when it was over, and sometimes he was very determined and refused to play at all.

And this night was one of the occasions on which he was firm.

The doctor, looking cautiously over the top of his book, watched the cat begin the performance. It started by gazing with an innocent expression at the dog where he lay with nose on paws and eyes wide open in the middle of the floor. Then it got up and made as though it meant to walk to the door, going deliberately and very softly. Flame's eyes followed it until it was beyond the range of sight, and then the cat turned sharply and began patting his tail tentatively with one paw. The tail moved slightly in reply, and Smoke changed paws and tapped it again. The dog, however, did not rise to play as was his wont, and the cat fell to patting it briskly with both paws. Flame still lay motionless.

This puzzled and bored the cat, and it went round and stared hard into its friend's face to see what was the matter. Perhaps some inarticulate message flashed from the dog's eyes into its own little brain, making it understand that the program for the night had better not begin with play. Perhaps it only realized that its friend was immovable. But, whatever the reason, its usual persistence thenceforward deserted it, and it made no further attempts at persuasion. Smoke yielded at once to the dog's mood; it sat down where it was and began to wash.

But the washing, the doctor noted, was by no means its real purpose; it only used it to mask something else; it stopped at the most busy and furious moments and began to stare about the room. Its thoughts wandered absurdly. It peered intently at the curtains; at the shadowy corners; at empty space above; leaving its body in curiously awkward positions for whole minutes together. Then it turned sharply and stared with a sudden signal of intelligence at the dog, and Flame at once rose somewhat stiffly to his feet and began to wander aimlessly and restlessly to and fro about the floor. Smoke followed him, padding quietly at his heels. Between them they made what seemed to be a deliberate search of the room.

And, here, as he watched them, noting carefully every detail of the performance over the top of his book, yet making no effort to interfere, it seemed to the doctor that the first beginnings of a faint distress betrayed themselves in the collie, and in the cat the stirrings of a vague excitement.

He observed them closely. The fog was thick in the air, and the tobacco smoke from his pipe added to its density; the furniture at the far end stood mistily, and where the shadows congregated in hanging clouds under the ceiling, it was difficult to see clearly at all; the lamplight only reached to a level of five feet from the floor, above which came layers of comparative darkness, so that the room appeared twice as lofty as it actually was. By means of the lamp and the fire, however, the carpet was everywhere clearly visible.

The animals made their silent tour of the floor, sometimes the dog leading, sometimes the cat; occasionally they looked at one another as though exchanging signals; and once or twice, in spite of the limited space, he lost sight of one or other among the fog and the shadows. Their curiosity, it appeared to him, was something more than the excitement lurking in the unknown territory of a strange room; yet, so far, it was impossible to test this, and he purposely kept his mind quietly receptive lest the smallest mental excitement on his part should communicate itself to the animals and thus destroy the value of their independent behaviour.

They made a very thorough journey, leaving no piece of furniture unexamined, or unsmelt. Flame led the way, walking slowly with lowered head, and Smoke followed demurely at his heels, making a transparent pretence of not being interested, yet missing nothing. And, at length, they returned, the old collie first, and came to rest on the mat before the fire. Flame rested his muzzle on his master's knee, smiling beatifically while he patted the yellow head and spoke his name; and Smoke, coming a little later, pretending he came by chance, looked from the empty saucer to his face, lapped up the milk when it was given him to the last drop, and then sprang upon his knees and curled round for the sleep it had fully earned and intended to enjoy.

Silence descended upon the room. Only the breathing of the dog upon the mat came through the deep stillness, like the pulse of time marking the minutes; and the steady drip, drip of the fog outside upon the window-ledges dismally testified to the inclemency of the night beyond. And the soft crashings of the coals as the fire settled down into the grate became less and less audible as the fire sank and the flames resigned their fierceness.

It was now well after eleven o'clock, and Dr. Silence devoted himself again to his book. He read the words on the printed page and took in their meaning superficially, yet without starting into life the correlations of thought and suggestion that should accompany interesting reading. Underneath, all the while, his mental energies were absorbed in watching, listening, waiting for what might come. He was not over sanguine himself, yet he did not wish to be taken by surprise. Moreover, the animals, his sensitive barometers, had incontinently gone to sleep.

After reading a dozen pages, however, he realized that his mind was really occupied in reviewing the features of Pender's extraordinary story, and that it was no longer necessary to steady his imagination by studying the dull paragraphs detailed in the pages before him. He laid down his book accordingly, and allowed his thoughts to dwell upon the features of the Case. Speculations as to the meaning, however, he rigorously suppressed, knowing that such thoughts would act upon his imagination like wind upon the glowing embers of a fire.

As the night wore on the silence grew deeper and deeper, and only at rare intervals he heard the sound of wheels on the main road a hundred yards away, where the horses went at a walking pace owing to the density of the fog. The echo of pedestrian footsteps no longer reached him, the clamour of occasional voices no longer came down the side street. The night, muffled by fog, shrouded by veils of ultimate mystery, hung about the haunted villa like a doom. Nothing in the house stirred. Stillness, in a thick blanket, lay over the upper storeys. Only the mist in the room grew more dense, he thought, and the damp cold more penetrating. Certainly, from time to time, he shivered.

The collie, now deep in slumber, moved occasionally, — grunted, sighed, or twitched his legs in dreams. Smoke lay on his knees, a pool of warm, black fur, only the closest observation detecting the movement of his sleek sides. It was difficult to distinguish exactly where his head and body joined in that circle of glistening hair; only a black satin nose and a tiny tip of pink tongue betrayed the secret.

Dr. Silence watched him, and felt comfortable. The collie's breathing was soothing. The fire was well built, and would burn for another two hours without attention. He was not conscious of the least nervousness. He particularly wished to remain in his ordinary and normal state of mind, and to force nothing. If sleep came naturally, he would let it come — and even welcome it. The coldness of the room, when the fire died down later, would be sure to wake him again; and it would then be time enough to carry these sleeping barometers up to bed. From various psychic premonitions he knew quite well that the night would not pass without adventure; but he did not wish to force its arrival; and he wished to remain normal, and let the animals remain normal, so that, when it came, it would be unattended by excitement or by any straining of the attention. Many experiments had made him wise. And, for the rest, he had no fear.

Accordingly, after a time, he did fall asleep as he had expected, and the last thing he remembered, before oblivion slipped up over his eyes like soft wool, was the picture of Flame stretching all four legs at once, and sighing noisily as he sought a more comfortable position for his paws and muzzle upon the mat.

*****

It was a good deal later when he became aware that a weight lay upon his chest, and that something was pencilling over his face and mouth. A soft touch on the cheek woke him. Something

57

was patting him.

He sat up with a jerk, and found himself staring straight into a pair of brilliant eyes, half green, half black. Smoke's face lay level with his own; and the cat had climbed up with its front paws upon his chest.

The lamp had burned low and the fire was nearly out, yet Dr. Silence saw in a moment that the cat was in an excited state. It kneaded with its front paws into his chest, shifting from one to the other. He felt them prodding against him. It lifted a leg very carefully and patted his cheek gingerly. Its fur, he saw, was standing ridgewise upon its back; the ears were flattened back somewhat; the tail was switching sharply. The cat, of course, had wakened him with a purpose, and the instant he realized this, he set it upon the arm of the chair and sprang up with a quick turn to face the empty room behind him. By some curious instinct, his arms of their own accord assumed an attitude of defence in front of him, as though to ward off something that threatened his safety. Yet nothing was visible. Only shapes of fog hung about rather heavily in the air, moving slightly to and fro.

His mind was now fully alert, and the last vestiges of sleep gone. He turned the lamp higher and peered about him. Two things he became aware of at once: one, that Smoke, while excited, was *pleasurably* excited; the other, that the collie was no longer visible upon the mat at his feet. He had crept away to the corner of the wall farthest from the window, and lay watching the room with wide-open eyes, in which lurked plainly something of alarm.

Something in the dog's behaviour instantly struck Dr. Silence as unusual, and, calling him by name, he moved across to pat him. Flame got up, wagged his tail, and came over slowly to the rug, uttering a low sound that was half growl, half whine. He was evidently perturbed about something, and his master was proceeding to administer comfort when his attention was suddenly drawn to the antics of his other four-footed companion, the cat.

And what he saw filled him with something like amazement.

Smoke had jumped down from the back of the arm-chair and now occupied the middle of the carpet, where, with tail erect and legs stiff as ramrods, it was steadily pacing backwards and forwards in a narrow space, uttering, as it did so, those curious little guttural sounds of pleasure that only an animal of the feline species knows how to make expressive of supreme happiness. Its stiffened legs and arched back made it appear larger than usual, and the black visage wore a smile of beatific joy. Its eyes blazed magnificently; it was in an ecstasy.

At the end of every few paces it turned sharply and stalked back again along the same line, padding softly, and purring like a roll of little muffled drums. It behaved precisely as though it were rubbing against the ankles of some one who remained invisible. A thrill ran down the doctor's spine as he stood and stared. His experiment was growing interesting at last.

He called the collie's attention to his friend's performance to see whether he too was aware of anything standing there upon the carpet, and the dog's behaviour was significant and corroborative. He came as far as his master's knees and then stopped dead, refusing to investigate closely. In vain Dr. Silence urged him; he wagged his tail, whined a little, and stood in a half-crouching attitude, staring alternately at the cat and at his master's face. He was, apparently, both puzzled and alarmed, and the whine went deeper and deeper down into his throat till it changed into an ugly snarl of awakening anger.

Then the doctor called to him in a tone of command he had never known to be disregarded; but still the dog, though springing up in response, declined to move nearer. He made tentative motions, pranced a little like a dog about to take to water, pretended to bark, and ran to and fro on the carpet. So far there was no actual fear in his manner, but he was uneasy and anxious, and nothing would induce him to go within touching distance of the walking cat. Once he made a complete circuit, but always carefully out of reach; and in the end he returned to his master's legs and rubbed vigorously against him. Flame did not like the performance at all: that much was quite clear.

For several minutes John Silence watched the performance of the cat with profound attention and without interfering. Then he called to the animal by name.

"Smoke, you mysterious beastie, what in the world are you about?" he said, in a coaxing tone.

The cat looked up at him for a moment, smiling in its ecstasy, blinking its eyes, but too happy to pause. He spoke to it again. He called to it several times, and each time it turned upon him its blazing eyes, drunk with inner delight, opening and shutting its lips, its body large and rigid with excitement. Yet it never for one instant paused in its short journeys to and fro.

He noted exactly what it did: it walked, he saw, the same number of paces each time, some six or seven steps, and then it turned sharply and retraced them. By the pattern of the great roses in the carpet he measured it. It kept to the same direction and the same line. It behaved precisely as though it were rubbing against something solid. Undoubtedly, there was something standing there on that strip of carpet, something invisible to the doctor, something that alarmed the dog, yet caused the cat unspeakable pleasure.

"Smokie!" he called again, "Smokie, you black mystery, what is it excites you so?"

Again the cat looked up at him for a brief second, and then continued its sentry-walk, blissfully happy, intensely preoccupied. And, for an instant, as he watched it, the doctor was aware that a faint uneasiness stirred in the depths of his own being, focusing itself for the moment upon this curious behaviour of the uncanny creature before him.

There rose in him quite a new realization of the mystery connected with the whole feline tribe, but especially with that common member of it, the domestic cat — their hidden lives, their strange aloofness, their incalculable subtlety. How utterly remote from anything that human beings understood lay the sources of their elusive activities. As he watched the indescribable bearing of the little creature mincing along the strip of carpet under his eyes, coquetting with the powers of darkness, welcoming, maybe, some fearsome visitor, there stirred in his heart a feeling strangely akin to awe. Its indifference to human kind, its serene superiority to the obvious, struck him forcibly with fresh meaning; so remote, so inaccessible seemed the secret purposes of its real life, so alien to the blundering honesty of other animals. Its absolute poise of bearing brought into his mind the opium-eater's words that "no dignity is perfect which does not at some point ally itself with the mysterious"; and he became suddenly aware that the presence of the dog in this foggy, haunted room on the top of Putney Hill was uncommonly welcome to him. He was glad to feel that Flame's dependable personality was with him. The savage growling at his heels was a pleasant sound. He was glad to hear it. That marching cat made him uneasy.

Finding that Smoke paid no further attention to his words, the doctor decided upon action. Would it rub against his leg, too? He would take it by surprise and see.

He stepped quickly forward and placed himself upon the exact strip of carpet where it walked.

But no cat is ever taken by surprise! The moment he occupied the space of the Intruder, setting his feet on the woven roses midway in the line of travel, Smoke suddenly stopped purring and sat down. It lifted up its face with the most innocent stare imaginable of its green eyes. He could have sworn it laughed. It was a perfect child again. In a single second it had resumed its simple, domestic manner; and it gazed at him in such a way that he almost felt Smoke was the normal being, and *his* was the eccentric behaviour that was being watched. It was consummate, the manner in which it brought about this change so easily and so quickly.

"Superb little actor!" he laughed in spite of himself, and stooped to stroke the shining black back. But, in a flash, as he touched its fur, the cat turned and spat at him viciously, striking at his hand with one paw. Then, with a hurried scutter of feet, it shot like a shadow across the floor and a moment later was calmly sitting over by the window-curtains washing its face as

61

though nothing interested it in the whole world but the cleanness of its cheeks and whiskers.

John Silence straightened himself up and drew a long breath. He realized that the performance was temporarily at an end. The collie, meanwhile, who had watched the whole proceeding with marked disapproval, had now lain down again upon the mat by the fire, no longer growling. It seemed to the doctor just as though something that had entered the room while he slept, alarming the dog, yet bringing happiness to the cat, had now gone out again, leaving all as it was before. Whatever it was that excited its blissful attentions had retreated for the moment.

He realized this intuitively. Smoke evidently realized it, too, for presently he deigned to march back to the fireplace and jump upon his master's knees. Dr. Silence, patient and determined, settled down once more to his book. The animals soon slept; the fire blazed cheerfully; and the cold fog from outside poured into the room through every available chink and crannie.

For a long time silence and peace reigned in the room and Dr. Silence availed himself of the quietness to make careful notes of what had happened. He entered for future use in other cases an exhaustive analysis of what he had observed, especially with regard to the effect upon the two animals. It is impossible here, nor would it be intelligible to the reader unversed in the knowledge of the region known to a scientifically trained psychic like Dr. Silence, to detail these observations. But to him it was clear, up to a certain point — and for the rest he must still wait and watch. So far, at least, he realized that while he slept in the chair — that is, while his will was dormant — the room had suffered intrusion from what he recognized as an intensely active Force, and might later be forced to acknowledge as something more than merely a blind force, namely, a distinct personality.

So far it had affected himself scarcely at all, but had acted directly upon the simpler organisms of the animals. It stimulated keenly the centres of the cat's psychic being, inducing a state of instant happiness (intensifying its consciousness probably in the same way a drug or stimulant intensifies that of a human being);

whereas it alarmed the less sensitive dog, causing it to feel a vague apprehension and distress.

His own sudden action and exhibition of energy had served to disperse it temporarily, yet he felt convinced — the indications were not lacking even while he sat there making notes — that it still remained near to him, conditionally if not spatially, and was, as it were, gathering force for a second attack.

And, further, he intuitively understood that the relations between the two animals had undergone a subtle change: that the cat had become immeasurably superior, confident, sure of itself in its own peculiar region, whereas Flame had been weakened by an attack he could not comprehend and knew not how to reply to. Though not yet afraid, he was defiant — ready to act against a fear that he felt to be approaching. He was no longer fatherly and protective towards the cat. Smoke held the key to the situation; and both he and the cat knew it.

Thus, as the minutes passed, John Silence sat and waited, keenly on the alert, wondering how soon the attack would be renewed, and at what point it would be diverted from the animals and directed upon himself.

The book lay on the floor beside him, his notes were complete. With one hand on the cat's fur, and the dog's front paws resting against his feet, the three of them dozed comfortably before the hot fire while the night wore on and the silence deepened towards midnight.

It was well after one o'clock in the morning when Dr. Silence turned the lamp out and lighted the candle preparatory to going up to bed. Then Smoke suddenly woke with a loud sharp purr and sat up. It neither stretched, washed nor turned: it listened. And the doctor, watching it, realized that a certain indefinable change had come about that very moment in the room. A swift readjustment of the forces within the four walls had taken place — a new disposition of their personal equations. The balance was destroyed, the former harmony gone. Smoke, most sensitive of barometers, had been the first to feel it, but the dog was not slow to follow suit, for on looking down he noted that Flame was no longer asleep. He was lying with eyes wide open, and that same instant he sat up on his great haunches and began to growl.

Dr. Silence was in the act of taking the matches to re-light the lamp when an audible movement in the room behind made him pause. Smoke leaped down from his knee and moved a few paces across the carpet. Then it stopped and stared fixedly; and the doctor stood up on the rug to watch.

As he rose the sound was repeated, and he discovered that it was not in the room as he first thought, but outside, and that it came from more directions than one. There was a rushing, sweeping noise against the window-panes, and simultaneously a sound of something brushing against the door — out in the hall. Smoke advanced sedately across the carpet, twitching his tail, and sat down within a foot of the door. The influence that had destroyed the harmonious conditions of the room had apparently moved in advance of its cause. Clearly, something was about to happen.

For the first time that night John Silence hesitated; the thought of that dark narrow hall-way, choked with fog, and destitute of human comfort, was unpleasant. He became aware of a faint creeping of his flesh. He knew, of course, that the actual opening of the door was not necessary to the invasion of the room that was about to take place, since neither doors nor windows, nor any other solid barriers could interpose an obstacle to what was seeking entrance. Yet the opening of the door would be significant and symbolic, and he distinctly shrank from it.

But for a moment only. Smoke, turning with a show of impatience, recalled him to his purpose, and he moved past the sitting, watching creature, and deliberately opened the door to its full width.

What subsequently happened, happened in the feeble and flickering light of the solitary candle on the mantelpiece.

Through the opened door he saw the hall, dimly lit and thick with fog. Nothing, of course, was visible — nothing but the hat-stand, the African spears in dark lines upon the wall and the high-backed wooden chair standing grotesquely underneath on the oilcloth floor. For one instant the fog seemed to move and thicken oddly; but he set that down to the score of the imagination. The door had opened upon nothing.

Yet Smoke apparently thought otherwise, and the deep growling of the collie from the mat at the back of the room seemed to confirm his judgment.

For, proud and self-possessed, the cat had again risen to his feet, and having advanced to the door, was now ushering some one slowly into the room. Nothing could have been more evident. He paced from side to side, bowing his little head with great *empressement* and holding his stiffened tail aloft like a flagstaff. He turned this way and that, mincing to and fro, and showing signs of supreme satisfaction. He was in his element. He welcomed the intrusion, and apparently reckoned that his companions, the doctor and the dog, would welcome it likewise.

The Intruder had returned for a second attack.

Dr. Silence moved slowly backwards and took up his position on the hearthrug, keying himself up to a condition of concentrated attention.

He noted that Flame stood beside him, facing the room, with body motionless, and head moving swiftly from side to side with a curious swaying movement. His eyes were wide open, his back rigid, his neck and jaws thrust forward, his legs tense and ready to leap. Savage, ready for attack or defence, yet dreadfully puzzled and perhaps already a little cowed, he stood and stared, the hair on his spine and sides positively bristling outwards as though a wind played through them. In the dim firelight he looked like a great yellow-haired wolf, silent, eyes shooting dark fire, exceedingly formidable. It was Flame, the terrible.

Smoke, meanwhile, advanced from the door towards the middle of the room, adopting the very slow pace of an invisible companion. A few feet away it stopped and began to smile and blink its eyes. There was something deliberately coaxing in its attitude as it stood there undecided on the carpet, clearly wishing to effect some sort of introduction between the Intruder and its canine friend and ally. It assumed its most winning manners, purring, smiling, looking persuasively from one to the other, and making quick tentative steps first in one direction and then in the other. There had always existed such perfect understanding between them in everything. Surely Flame would appreciate Smoke's intentions now, and acquiesce.

But the old collie made no advances. He bared his teeth, lifting his lips till the gums showed, and stood stockstill with fixed eyes and heaving sides. The doctor moved a little farther back, watching intently the smallest movement, and it was just then he divined suddenly from the cat's behaviour and attitude that it was not only a single companion it had ushered into the room, but *several*. It kept crossing over from one to the other, looking up at each in turn. It sought to win over the dog to friendliness with them all. The original Intruder had come back with reinforcements. And at the same time he further realized that the Intruder was something more than a blindly acting force, impersonal though destructive. It was a Personality, and moreover a great personality. And it was accompanied for the purposes of assistance by a host of other personalities, minor in degree, but similar in kind.

He braced himself in the corner against the mantelpiece and waited, his whole being roused to defence, for he was now fully aware that the attack had spread to include himself as well as the animals, and he must be on the alert. He strained his eyes through the foggy atmosphere, trying in vain to see what the cat and dog saw; but the candlelight threw an uncertain and flickering light across the room and his eyes discerned nothing. On the floor Smoke moved softly in front of him like a black shadow, his eyes gleaming as he turned his head, still trying with many insinuating gestures and much purring to bring about the introductions he desired.

But it was all in vain. Flame stood riveted to one spot, motionless as a figure carved in stone.

Some minutes passed, during which only the cat moved, and there came a sharp change. Flame began to back towards the wall. He moved his head from side to side as he went, sometimes turning to snap at something almost behind him. *They* were advancing upon him, trying to surround him. His distress became very marked from now onwards, and it seemed to the doctor that his anger merged into genuine terror and became overwhelmed by it. The savage growl sounded perilously like a whine, and more than once he tried to dive past his master's legs, as though hunting for a way of escape. He was trying to avoid something that everywhere blocked the way.

This terror of the indomitable fighter impressed the doctor enormously; yet also painfully; stirring his impatience; for he had never before seen the dog show signs of giving in, and it distressed him to witness it. He knew, however, that he was not giving in easily, and understood that it was really impossible for him to gauge the animal's sensations properly at all. What Flame felt, and saw, must be terrible indeed to turn him all at once into a coward. He faced something that made him afraid of more than his life merely. The doctor spoke a few quick words of encouragement to him, and stroked the bristling hair. But without much success. The collie seemed already beyond the reach of comfort such as that, and the collapse of the old dog followed indeed very speedily after this.

And Smoke, meanwhile, remained behind, watching the advance, but not joining in it; sitting, pleased and expectant, considering that all was going well and as it wished. It was kneading on the carpet with its front paws — slowly, laboriously, as though its feet were dipped in treacle. The sound its claws made as they caught in the threads was distinctly audible. It was still smiling, blinking, purring.

Suddenly the collie uttered a poignant short bark and leaped heavily to one side. His bared teeth traced a line of whiteness through the gloom. The next instant he dashed past his master's legs, almost upsetting his balance, and shot out into the room, where he went blundering wildly against walls and furniture. But that bark was significant; the doctor had heard it before and knew what it meant: for it was the cry of the fighter against odds and it meant that the old beast had found his courage again. Possibly it was only the courage of despair, but at any rate the fighting would be terrific. And Dr. Silence understood, too, that he dared not interfere. Flame must fight his own enemies in his own way.

But the cat, too, had heard that dreadful bark; and it, too, had understood. This was more than it had bargained for. Across the dim shadows of that haunted room there must have passed some secret signal of distress between the animals. Smoke stood up and looked swiftly about him. He uttered a piteous meow and trotted smartly away into the greater darkness by the windows. What his object was only those endowed with the spirit-like intelligence of cats might know. But, at any rate, he had at last ranged himself on the side of his friend. And the little beast meant business.

At the same moment the collie managed to gain the door. The doctor saw him rush through into the hall like a flash of yellow light. He shot across the oilcloth, and tore up the stairs, but in another second he appeared again, flying down the steps and landing at the bottom in a tumbling heap, whining, cringing, terrified. The doctor saw him slink back into the room again and crawl round by the wall towards the cat. Was, then, even the staircase occupied? Did *They* stand also in the hall? Was the whole house crowded from floor to ceiling?

The thought came to add to the keen distress he felt at the sight of the collie's discomfiture. And, indeed, his own personal distress had increased in a marked degree during the past minutes, and continued to increase steadily to the climax. He recognized that the drain on his own vitality grew steadily, and that the attack was now directed against himself even more than against the defeated dog, and the too much deceived cat.

It all seemed so rapid and uncalculated after that — the events that took place in this little modern room at the top of Putney Hill between midnight and sunrise — that Dr. Silence was hardly able to follow and remember it all. It came about with such uncanny swiftness and terror; the light was so uncertain; the movements of the black cat so difficult to follow on the dark carpet, and the doctor himself so weary and taken by surprise —

that he found it almost impossible to observe accurately, or to recall afterwards precisely what it was he had seen or in what order the incidents had taken place. He never could understand what defect of vision on his part made it seem as though the cat had duplicated itself at first, and then increased indefinitely, so that there were at least a dozen of them darting silently about the floor, leaping softly on to chairs and tables, passing like shadows from the open door to the end of the room, all black as sin, with brilliant green eyes flashing fire in all directions. It was like the reflections from a score of mirrors placed round the walls at different angles. Nor could he make out at the time why the size of the room seemed to have altered, grown much larger, and why it extended away behind him where ordinarily the wall should have been. The snarling of the enraged and terrified collie sounded sometimes so far away; the ceiling seemed to have raised itself so much higher than before, and much of the furniture had changed in appearance and shifted marvellously.

It was all so confused and confusing, as though the little room he knew had become merged and transformed into the dimensions of quite another chamber, that came to him, with its host of cats and its strange distances, in a sort of vision.

But these changes came about a little later, and at a time when his attention was so concentrated upon the proceedings of Smoke and the collie, that he only observed them, as it were, subconsciously. And the excitement, the flickering candlelight, the distress he felt for the collie, and the distorting atmosphere of fog were the poorest possible allies to careful observation.

At first he was only aware that the dog was repeating his short dangerous bark from time to time, snapping viciously at the empty air, a foot or so from the ground. Once, indeed, he sprang upwards and forwards, working furiously with teeth and paws, and with a noise like wolves fighting, but only to dash back the next minute against the wall behind him. Then, after lying still for a bit, he rose to a crouching position as though to spring again, snarling horribly and making short half-circles with lowered head. And Smoke all the while meowed piteously by the window as though trying to draw the attack upon himself.

Then it was that the rush of the whole dreadful business seemed to turn aside from the dog and direct itself upon his own person. The collie had made another spring and fallen back with a crash into the corner, where he made noise enough in his savage rage to waken the dead before he fell to whining and then finally lay still. And directly afterwards the doctor's own distress became intolerably acute. He had made a half movement forward to come to the rescue when a veil that was denser than mere fog seemed to drop down over the scene, draping room, walls, animals and fire in a mist of darkness and folding also about his own mind. Other forms moved silently across the field of vision, forms that he recognized from previous experiments, and welcomed not. Unholy thoughts began to crowd into his brain, sinister suggestions of evil presented themselves seductively. Ice seemed to settle about his heart, and his mind trembled. He began to lose memory — memory of his identity, of where he was, of what he ought to do. The very foundations of his strength were shaken. His will seemed paralysed.

And it was then that the room filled with this horde of cats, all dark as the night, all silent, all with lamping eyes of green fire. The dimensions of the place altered and shifted. He was in a much larger space. The whining of the dog sounded far away, and all about him the cats flew busily to and fro, silently playing their tearing, rushing game of evil, weaving the pattern of their dark purpose upon the floor. He strove hard to collect himself and remember the words of power he had made use of before in similar dread positions where his dangerous practice had sometimes led; but he could recall nothing consecutively; a mist lay over his mind and memory; he felt dazed and his forces scattered. The deeps within were too troubled for healing power to come out of them.

It was glamour, of course, he realized afterwards, the strong glamour thrown upon his imagination by some powerful personality behind the veil; but at the time he was not sufficiently aware of this and, as with all true glamour, was unable to grasp where the true ended and the false began. He was caught momentarily in the same vortex that had sought to lure the cat to destruction

70

through its delight, and threatened utterly to overwhelm the dog through its terror.

There came a sound in the chimney behind him like wind booming and tearing its way down. The windows rattled. The candle flickered and went out. The glacial atmosphere closed round him with the cold of death, and a great rushing sound swept by overhead as though the ceiling had lifted to a great height. He heard the door shut. Far away it sounded. He felt lost, shelterless in the depths of his soul. Yet still he held out and resisted while the climax of the fight came nearer and nearer.... He had stepped into the stream of forces awakened by Pender and he knew that he must withstand them to the end or come to a conclusion that it was not good for a man to come to. Something from the region of utter cold was upon him.

And then quite suddenly, through the confused mists about him, there slowly rose up the Personality that had been all the time directing the battle. Some force entered his being that shook him as the tempest shakes a leaf, and close against his eyes — clean level with his face — he found himself staring into the wreck of a vast dark Countenance, a countenance that was terrible even in its ruin.

For ruined it was, and terrible it was, and the mark of spiritual evil was branded everywhere upon its broken features. Eyes, face and hair rose level with his own, and for a space of time he never could properly measure, or determine, these two, a man and a woman, looked straight into each other's visages and down into each other's hearts.

And John Silence, the soul with the good, unselfish motive, held his own against the dark discarnate woman whose motive was pure evil, and whose soul was on the side of the Dark Powers.

It was the climax that touched the depth of power within him and began to restore him slowly to his own. He was conscious, of course, of effort, and yet it seemed no superhuman one, for he had recognized the character of his opponent's power, and he called upon the good within him to meet and overcome it. The inner forces stirred and trembled in response to his call. They did not at first come readily as was their habit, for under the spell of glamour they had already been diabolically lulled into inactivity, but come they eventually did, rising out of the inner spiritual nature he had learned with so much time and pain to awaken to life. And power and confidence came with them. He began to breathe deeply and regularly, and at the same time to absorb into himself the forces opposed to him, and to *turn them to his account*. By ceasing to resist, and allowing the deadly stream to pour into him unopposed, he used the very power supplied by his adversary and thus enormously increased his own.

For this spiritual alchemy he had learned. He understood that force ultimately is everywhere one and the same; it is the motive behind that makes it good or evil; and his motive was entirely unselfish. He knew — provided he was not first robbed of self-control — how vicariously to absorb these evil radiations into himself and change them magically into his own good purposes. And, since his motive was pure and his soul fearless, they could not work him harm.

Thus he stood in the main stream of evil unwittingly attracted by Pender, deflecting its course upon himself; and after passing through the purifying filter of his own unselfishness these energies could only add to his store of experience, of knowledge, and therefore of power. And, as his self-control returned to him, he gradually accomplished this purpose, even though trembling while he did so.

Yet the struggle was severe, and in spite of the freezing chill of the air, the perspiration poured down his face. Then, by slow degrees, the dark and dreadful countenance faded, the glamour passed from his soul, the normal proportions returned to walls and ceiling, the forms melted back into the fog, and the whirl of rushing shadow-cats disappeared whence they came.

And with the return of the consciousness of his own identity John Silence was restored to the full control of his own will-power. In a deep, modulated voice he began to utter certain rhythmical sounds that slowly rolled through the air like a rising sea, filling the room with powerful vibratory activities that whelmed all irregularities of lesser vibrations in its own swelling tone. He made certain sigils, gestures and movements at the same time. For several minutes he continued to utter these words, until at length the growing volume dominated the whole room and mastered the manifestation of all that opposed it. For just as he understood the spiritual alchemy that can transmute evil forces by raising them into higher channels, so he knew from long study the occult use of sound, and its direct effect upon the plastic region wherein the powers of spiritual evil work their fell purposes. Harmony was restored first of all to his own soul, and thence to the room and all its occupants.

And, after himself, the first to recognize it was the old dog lying in his corner. Flame began suddenly uttering sounds of pleasure, that "something" between a growl and a grunt that dogs make upon being restored to their master's confidence. Dr. Silence heard the thumping of the collie's tail against the ground. And the grunt and the thumping touched the depth of affection in the man's heart, and gave him some inkling of what agonies the dumb creature had suffered.

Next, from the shadows by the window, a somewhat shrill purring announced the restoration of the cat to its normal state. Smoke was advancing across the carpet. He seemed very pleased with himself, and smiled with an expression of supreme innocence. He was no shadow-cat, but real and full of his usual and perfect self-possession. He marched along, picking his way delicately, but with a stately dignity that suggested his ancestry with the majesty of Egypt. His eyes no longer glared; they shone steadily before him; they radiated, not excitement, but knowledge. Clearly he was anxious to make amends for the mischief to which he had unwittingly lent himself owing to his subtle and electric constitution.

Still uttering his sharp high purrings he marched up to his master and rubbed vigorously against his legs. Then he stood on his hind feet and pawed his knees and stared beseechingly up into his face. He turned his head towards the corner where the collie still lay, thumping his tail feebly and pathetically.

John Silence understood. He bent down and stroked the creature's living fur, noting the line of bright blue sparks that followed the motion of his hand down its back. And then they advanced together towards the corner where the dog was.

Smoke went first and put his nose gently against his friend's muzzle, purring while he rubbed, and uttering little soft sounds of affection in his throat. The doctor lit the candle and brought it over. He saw the collie lying on its side against the wall; it was utterly exhausted, and foam still hung about its jaws. Its tail and eyes responded to the sound of its name, but it was evidently very weak and overcome. Smoke continued to rub against its cheek and nose and eyes, sometimes even standing on its body and kneading into the thick yellow hair. Flame replied from time to time by little licks of the tongue, most of them curiously misdirected.

But Dr. Silence felt intuitively that something disastrous had happened, and his heart was wrung. He stroked the dear body, feeling it over for bruises or broken bones, but finding none. He fed it with what remained of the sandwiches and milk, but the creature clumsily upset the saucer and lost the sandwiches between its paws, so that the doctor had to feed it with his own hand. And all the while Smoke meowed piteously.

Then John Silence began to understand. He went across to the farther side of the room and called aloud to it.

"Flame, old man! come!"

At any other time the dog would have been upon him in an instant, barking and leaping to the shoulder. And even now he got up, though heavily and awkwardly, to his feet. He started to run, wagging his tail more briskly. He collided first with a chair, and then ran straight into a table. Smoke trotted close at his side, trying his very best to guide him. But it was useless. Dr. Silence had to lift him up into his own arms and carry him like a baby. For he was blind.

III

It was a week later when John Silence called to see the author in his new house, and found him well on the way to recovery and already busy again with his writing. The haunted look had left his eyes, and he seemed cheerful and confident.

"Humour restored?" laughed the doctor, as soon as they were comfortably settled in the room overlooking the Park.

"I've had no trouble since I left that dreadful place," returned Pender gratefully; "and thanks to you — "

The doctor stopped him with a gesture.

"Never mind that," he said, "we'll discuss your new plans afterwards, and my scheme for relieving you of the house and helping you settle elsewhere. Of course it must be pulled down, for it's not fit for any sensitive person to live in, and any other tenant might be afflicted in the same way you were. Although, personally, I think the evil has exhausted itself by now."

He told the astonished author something of his experiences in it with the animals.

"I don't pretend to understand," Pender said, when the account was finished, "but I and my wife are intensely relieved to be free of it all. Only I must say I should like to know something of the former history of the house. When we took it six months ago I heard no word against it."

Dr. Silence drew a typewritten paper from his pocket.

"I can satisfy your curiosity to some extent," he said, running his eye over the sheets, and then replacing them in his coat; "for by my secretary's investigations I have been able to check certain information obtained in the hypnotic trance by a 'sensitive' who helps me in such cases. The former occupant who haunted you appears to have been a woman of singularly atrocious life and character who finally suffered death by hanging, after a series of crimes that appalled the whole of England and only came to light by the merest chance. She came to her end in the year 1798, for it was not this particular house she lived in, but a much larger one that then stood upon the site it now occupies, and was then, of course, not in London, but in the country. She was a person of intellect, possessed of a powerful, trained will, and of consummate audacity, and I am convinced availed herself of the resources of the lower magic to attain her ends. This goes far to explain the virulence of the attack upon yourself, and why she is still able to carry on after death the evil practices that formed her main purpose during life."

"You think that after death a soul can still consciously direct — " gasped the author.

"I think, as I told you before, that the forces of a powerful personality may still persist after death in the line of their original momentum," replied the doctor; "and that strong thoughts and purposes can still react upon suitably prepared brains long after their originators have passed away.

"If you knew anything of magic," he pursued, "you would know that thought is dynamic, and that it may call into existence forms and pictures that may well exist for hundreds of years. For, not far removed from the region of our human life, is another region where floats the waste and drift of all the centuries, the limbo of the shells of the dead; a densely populated region crammed with horror and abomination of all descriptions, and sometimes galvanized into active life again by the will of a trained manipulator, a mind versed in the practices of lower magic. That this woman understood its vile commerce, I am persuaded, and the forces she set going during her life have simply been accumulating ever since, and would have continued to do so had they not been drawn down upon yourself, and afterwards discharged and satisfied through me.

"Anything might have brought down the attack, for, besides drugs, there are certain violent emotions, certain moods of the soul, certain spiritual fevers, if I may so call them, which directly open the inner being to a cognizance of this astral region I have mentioned. In your case it happened to be a peculiarly potent drug that did it."

"But now, tell me," he added, after a pause, handing to the perplexed author a pencil-drawing he had made of the dark countenance that had appeared to him during the night on Putney Hill — "tell me if you recognize this face?"

Pender looked at the drawing closely, greatly astonished. He shuddered as he looked.

"Undoubtedly," he said, "it is the face I kept trying to draw — dark, with the great mouth and jaw, and the drooping eye. That is the woman."

Dr. Silence then produced from his pocket-book an old-fashioned woodcut of the same person which his secretary had unearthed from the records of the Newgate Calendar. The woodcut and the pencil drawing were two different aspects of the same dreadful visage. The men compared them for some moments in silence.

"It makes me thank God for the limitations of our senses," said Pender quietly, with a sigh; "continuous clairvoyance must be a sore affliction."

"It is indeed," returned John Silence significantly, "and if all the people nowadays who claim to be clairvoyant were really so, the statistics of suicide and lunacy would be considerably higher than they are. It is little wonder," he added, "that your sense of humour was clouded, with the mind-forces of that dead monster trying to use your brain for their dissemination. You have had an interesting adventure, Mr. Felix Pender, and, let me add, a fortunate escape."

The author was about to renew his thanks when there came a sound of scratching at the door, and the doctor sprang up quickly.

"It's time for me to go. I left my dog on the step, but I suppose — "

Before he had time to open the door, it had yielded to the pressure behind it and flew wide open to admit a great yellow-haired collie. The dog, wagging his tail and contorting his whole body with delight, tore across the floor and tried to leap up upon his owner's breast. And there was laughter and happiness in the old eyes; for they were clear again as the day.

Algernon Blackwood.

THE AFFLICTIONS OF AN ENGLISH CAT

When the report of your first meeting arrived in London, O! French Animals, it caused the hearts of the friends of Animal Reform to beat faster. In my own humble experience, I have so many proofs of the superiority of Beasts over Man that in my character of an English Cat I see the occasion, long awaited, of publishing the story of my life, in order to show how my poor soul has been tortured by the hypocritical laws of England. On two occasions, already, some Mice, whom I have made a vow to respect since the bill passed by your august parliament, have taken me to Colburn's, where, observing old ladies, spinsters of uncertain years, and even young married women, correcting proofs, I have asked myself why, having claws, I should not make use of them in a similar manner. One never knows what women think, especially the women who write, while a Cat, victim of English perfidy, is interested to say more than she thinks, and her profuseness may serve to compensate for what these ladies do not say. I am ambitious to be the Mrs. Inchbald of Cats and I beg you to have consideration for my noble efforts, O! French Cats, among whom has risen the noblest house of our race, that of Puss in Boots, eternal type of Advertiser, whom so many men have imitated but to whom no one has yet erected a monument.

I was born at the home of a parson in Catshire, near the little town of Miaulbury. My mother's fecundity condemned nearly all her infants to a cruel fate, because, as you know, the cause of the maternal intemperance of English cats, who threaten to populate the whole world, has not yet been decided. Toms and females each insist it is due to their own amiability and respective virtues. But impertinent observers have remarked that Cats in England are required to be so boringly proper that this is their only distraction. Others pretend that herein may lie concealed great questions of commerce and politics, having to do with the English rule of India, but these matters are not for my paws to write of and I leave them to the *Edinburgh-Review*. I was not drowned with the others on account of the whiteness of my robe. Also I was named Beauty. Alas! the parson, who had a wife and eleven daughters, was too poor to keep me. An elderly female noticed that I had an affection for the parson's Bible; I slept on it all the time, not because I was religious, but because it was the only clean spot I could find in the house. She believed, perhaps, that I belonged to the sect of sacred animals which had already furnished the she-ass of Balaam, and took me away with her. I was only two months old at this time. This old woman, who gave evenings for which she sent out cards inscribed *Tea and Bible*, tried to communicate to me the fatal science of the daughters of Eve. Her method, which consisted in delivering long lectures on personal dignity and on the obligations due the world, was a very successful one. In order to avoid these lectures one submitted to martyrdom.

One morning I, a poor little daughter of Nature, attracted by a bowl of cream, covered by a muffin, knocked the muffin off with my paw, and lapped the cream. Then in joy, and perhaps also on account of the weakness of my young organs, I delivered myself on the waxed floor to the imperious need which young Cats feel. Perceiving the proofs of what she called my intemperance and my faults of education, the old woman seized me and whipped me vigorously with a birchrod, protesting that she would make me a lady or she would abandon me.

"Permit me to give you a lesson in gentility," she said. "Understand, Miss Beauty, that English Cats veil natural acts, which are opposed to the laws of English respectability, in the most profound mystery, and banish all that is improper, applying to the creature, as you have heard the Reverend Doctor Simpson say, the laws made by God for the creation. Have you ever seen the Earth behave itself indecently? Learn to suffer a thousand deaths rather than reveal your desires; in this suppression consists the virtue of the saints. The greatest privilege of Cats is to depart with the grace that characterizes your actions, and let no one know where you are going to make your little toilets. Thus you expose yourself only when you are beautiful. Deceived by appearances, everybody will take you for an angel. In the future when such a desire seizes you, look out of the window, give the impression that you desire to go for a walk, then run to a copse or to the gutter."

As a simple Cat of good sense, I found much hypocrisy in this doctrine, but I was so young!

"And when I am in the gutter?" thought I, looking at the old woman.

"Once alone, and sure of not being seen by anybody, well, Beauty, you can sacrifice respectability with much more charm because you have been discreet in public. It is in the observance of this very precept that the perfection of the moral English shines the brightest: they occupy themselves exclusively with appearances, this world being, alas, only illusion and deception."

I admit that these disguises were revolting to all my animal good sense, but on account of the whipping, it seemed preferable to understand that exterior propriety was all that was demanded of an English Cat. From this moment I accustomed myself to conceal the titbits that I loved under the bed. Nobody ever saw me eat, or drink, or make my toilet. I was regarded as the pearl of Cats.

Now I had occasion to observe those stupid men who are called savants. Among the doctors and others who were friends of my mistress, there was this Simpson, a fool, a son of a rich landowner, who was waiting for a bequest, and who, to deserve it, explained all animal actions by religious theories. He saw me one evening lapping milk from a saucer and complimented the old woman on the manner in which I had been bred, seeing me lick first the edges of the saucer and gradually diminish the circle of fluid.

"See," he said, "how in saintly company all becomes perfection: Beauty understands eternity, because she describes the circle which is its emblem in lapping her milk."

Conscience obliges me to state that the aversion of Cats to wetting their fur was the only reason for my fashion of drinking, but we will always be badly understood by the savants who are much more preoccupied in showing their own wit, than in discovering ours.

When the ladies or the gentlemen lifted me to pass their

hands over my snowy back to make the sparks fly from my hair, the old woman remarked with pride, "You can hold her without having any fear for your dress; she is admirably well-bred!" Everybody said I was an angel; I was loaded with delicacies, but I assure you that I was profoundly bored. I was well aware of the fact that a young female Cat of the neighbourhood had run away with a Tom. This word, Tom, caused my soul a suffering which nothing could alleviate, not even the compliments I received, or rather that my mistress lavished on herself.

"Beauty is entirely moral; she is a little angel," she said. "Although she is very beautiful she has the air of not knowing it. She never looks at anybody, which is the height of a fine aristocratic education. When she does look at anybody it is with that perfect indifference which we demand of our young girls, but which we obtain only with great difficulty. She never intrudes herself unless you call her; she never jumps on you with familiarity; nobody ever sees her eat, and certainly that monster of a Lord Byron would have adored her. Like a tried and true Englishwoman she loves tea, sits, gravely calm, while the Bible is being explained, and thinks badly of nobody, a fact which permits one to speak freely before her. She is simple, without affectation, and has no desire for jewels. Give her a ring and she will not keep it. Finally, she does not imitate the vulgarity of the hunter. She loves her home and remains there so perfectly tranquil that at times you would believe that she was a mechanical Cat made at Birmingham or Manchester, which is the *ne plus ultra* of the finest education."

What these men and old women call education is the custom of dissimulating natural manners, and when they have completely depraved us they say that we are well-bred. One evening my mistress begged one of the young ladies to sing. When this girl went to the piano and began to sing I recognized at once an Irish melody that I had heard in my youth, and I remembered that I also was a musician. So I merged my voice with hers, but I received some raps on the head while she received compliments. I was revolted by this sovereign injustice and ran away to the garret. Sacred love of country! What a delicious night! I at last knew what the roof was. I heard Toms sing hymns to their mates, and these adorable elegies made me feel ashamed of the hypocrisies my mistress had forced upon me. Soon some of the Cats observed me and appeared to take offence at my presence, when a Tom with shaggy hair, a magnificent beard, and a fine figure, came to look at me and said to the company, "It's only a child!" At these condescending words, I bounded about on the tiles, moving with that agility which distinguishes us; I fell on my paws in that flexible fashion which no other animal knows how to imitate in order to show that I was no child. But these calineries were a pure waste of time. "When will some one serenade me?" I asked myself. The aspect of these haughty Toms, their melodies, that the human voice could never hope to rival, had moved me profoundly, and were the cause of my inventing little lyrics that I sang on the stairs. But an event of tremendous importance was about to occur which tore me violently from this innocent life. I went to London with a niece of my mistress, a rich heiress who adored me, who kissed me, caressed me with a kind of madness, and who pleased me so much that I became attached to her, against all the habits of our race. We were never separated and I was able to observe the great world of London during the season. It was there that I studied the perversity of English manners, which have power even over the beasts, that I became acquainted with that cant which Byron cursed and of which I am the victim as well as he, but without having enjoyed my hours of leisure.

Arabella, my mistress, was a young person like many others in England; she was not sure whom she wanted for a husband. The absolute liberty that is permitted girls in choosing a husband drives them nearly crazy, especially when they recall that English custom does not sanction intimate conversation after marriage. I was far from dreaming that the London Cats had adopted this severity, that the English laws would be cruelly applied to me, and that I would be a victim of the court at the terrible Doctors' Commons. Arabella was charming to all the men she met, and every one of them believed that he was going to marry this beautiful girl, but when an affair threatened to terminate in wedlock, she would find some pretext for a break, conduct which did not seem very respectable to me. "Marry a bow-legged man! Never!"

she said of one. "As to that little fellow he is snub-nosed." Men were all so much alike to me that I could not understand this uncertainty founded on purely physical differences.

Finally one day an old English Peer, seeing me, said to her: "You have a beautiful Cat. She resembles you. She is white, she is young, she should have a husband. Let me bring her a magnificent Angora that I have at home."

Three days later the Peer brought in the handsomest Tom of the Peerage. Puff, with a black coat, had the most magnificent eyes, green and yellow, but cold and proud. The long silky hair of his tail, remarkable for its yellow rings, swept the carpet. Perhaps he came from the imperial house of Austria, because, as you see, he wore the colours. His manners were those of a Cat who had seen the court and the great world. His severity, in the matter of carrying himself, was so great that he would not scratch his head were anybody present. Puff had travelled on the continent. To sum up, he was so remarkably handsome that he had been, it was said, caressed by the Queen of England. Simple and naïve as I was I leaped at his neck to engage him in play, but he refused under the pretext that we were being watched. I then perceived that this English Cat Peer owed this forced and fictitious gravity that in England is called respectability to age and to intemperance at table. His weight, that men admired, interfered with his movements. Such was the true reason for his not responding to my pleasant advances. Calm and cold he sat on his unnamable, agitating his beard, looking at me and at times closing his eyes. In the society world of English Cats, Puff was the richest kind of catch for a Cat born at a parson's. He had two valets in his service; he ate from Chinese porcelain, and he drank only black tea. He drove in a carriage in Hyde Park and had been to parliament.

My mistress kept him. Unknown to me, all the feline population of London learned that Miss Beauty from Catshire had married Puff, marked with the colours of Austria. During the night I heard a concert in the street. Accompanied by my lord, who, according to his taste, walked slowly, I descended. We found the Cats of the Peerage, who had come to congratulate me and to ask me to join their Ratophile Society. They explained that nothing was more common than running after Rats and Mice. The words, shocking, vulgar, were constantly on their lips. To conclude, they had formed, for the glory of the country, a Temperance Society. A few nights later my lord and I went on the roof of Almack's to hear a grey Cat speak on the subject. In his exhortation, which was constantly supported by cries of "Hear! Hear!" he proved that Saint Paul in writing about charity had the Cats of England in mind. It was then the special duty of the English, who could go from one end of the world to the other on their ships without fear of the sea, to spread the principles of the *morale ratophile*. As a matter of fact English Cats were already preaching the doctrines of the Society, based on the hygienic discoveries of science. When Rats and Mice were dissected little distinction could be found between them and Cats; the oppression of one race by the other then was opposed to the Laws of Beasts, which are stronger even than the Laws of Men. "They are our brothers," he continued. And he painted such a vivid picture of the suffering of a Rat in the jaws of a Cat that I burst into tears.

Observing that I was deceived by this speech, Lord Puff confided to me that England expected to do an immense trade in Rats and Mice; that if the Cats would eat no more, Rats would be England's best product; that there was always a practical reason concealed behind English morality; and that the alliance between morality and trade was the only alliance on which England really counted.

Puff appeared to me to be too good a politician ever to make a satisfactory husband.

A country Cat made the observation that on the continent, especially at Paris, near the fortifications, Tom Cats were sacrificed daily by the Catholics. Somebody interrupted with the cry of "Question!" Added to these cruel executions was the frightful slander of passing the brave animals off for Rabbits, a lie and a barbarity which he attributed to an ignorance of the true Anglican religion which did not permit lying and cheating except in the government, foreign affairs, and the cabinet.

He was treated as a radical and a dreamer. "We are here in

the interests of the Cats of England, not in those of continental Cats!" cried a fiery Tory Tom. Puff went to sleep. Just as the assembly was breaking up a young Cat from the French embassy, whose accent proclaimed his nationality, addressed me these delicious words:

"Dear Beauty, it will be an eternity before Nature forms another Cat as perfect as you. The cashmere of Persia and the Indies is like camel's hair when it is compared to your fine and brilliant silk. You exhale a perfume which is the concentrated essence of the felicity of the angels, an odour I have detected in the salon of the Prince de Talleyrand, which I left to come to this stupid meeting. The fire of your eyes illuminates the night! Your ears would be entirely perfect if they would listen to my supplications. There is not a rose in England as rose as the rose flesh which borders your little rose mouth. A fisherman would search in vain in the depths of Ormus for pearls of the quality of your teeth. Your dear face, fine and gracious, is the loveliest that England has produced. Near to your celestial robe the snow of the Alps would seem to be red. Ah! those coats which are only to be seen in your fogs! Softly and gracefully your paws bear your body which is the culmination of the miracles of creation, but your tail, the subtle interpreter of the beating of your heart, surpasses it. Yes! never was there such an exquisite curve, more correct roundness. No Cat ever moved more delicately. Come away from this old fool of a Puff, who sleeps like an English Peer in parliament, who besides is a scoundrel who has sold himself to the Whigs, and who, owing to a too long sojourn at Bengal, has lost everything that can please a Cat."

Then, without having the air of looking at him, I took in the appearance of this charming French Tom. He was a careless little rogue and not in any respect like an English Cat. His cavalier manner as well as his way of shaking his ear stamped him as a gay bachelor without a care. I avow that I was weary of the solemnity of English Cats, and of their purely practical propriety. Their respectability, especially, seemed ridiculous to me. The excessive naturalness of this badly groomed Cat surprised me in its violent contrast to all that I had seen in London. Besides my life was so strictly regulated, I knew so well what I had to count on for the rest of my days, that I welcomed the promise of the unexpected in the physiognomy of this French Cat. My whole life appeared insipid to me. I comprehended that I could live on the roofs with an amazing creature who came from that country where the inhabitants consoled themselves for the victories of the greatest English general by these words:

Malbrouk s'en va-t-en guerre,
Mironton, ton, ton, MIRONTAINE!

Nevertheless I awakened my lord, told him how late it was, and suggested that we ought to go in. I gave no sign of having listened to this declaration, and my apparent insensibility petrified Brisquet. He remained behind, more surprised than ever because he considered himself handsome. I learned later that it was an easy matter for him to seduce most Cats. I examined him through a corner of my eye: he ran away with little bounds, returned, leaping the width of the street, then jumped back again, like a French Cat in despair. A true Englishman would have been decent enough not to let me see how he felt.

Some days later my lord and I were stopping in the magnificent house of the old Peer; then I went in the carriage for a drive in Hyde Park. We ate only chicken bones, fishbones, cream, milk, and chocolate. However heating this diet might prove to others my so-called husband remained sober. He was respectable even in his treatment of me. Generally he slept from seven in the evening at the whist table on the knees of his Grace. On this account my soul received no satisfaction and I pined away. This condition was aggravated by a little affection of the intestines occasioned by pure herring oil (the Port Wine of English Cats), which Puff used, and which made me very ill. My mistress sent for a physician who had graduated at Edinburgh after having studied a long time in Paris. Having diagnosed my malady he promised my mistress that he would cure me the next day. He returned, as a matter of fact, and took an instrument of French manufacture out of his pocket. I felt a kind of fright on perceiving a barrel of white metal terminating in a slender tube. At the sight of this mechanism, which the doctor exhibited with satisfaction, Their Graces blushed, became irritable, and muttered several fine sentiments about the dignity of the English: for instance that the Catholics of old England were more distinguished for their opinions of this infamous instrument than for their opinions of the Bible. The Duke added that at Paris the French unblushingly made an exhibition of it in their national theatre in a comedy by Molière, but that in London a watchman would not dare pronounce its name.

"Give her some calomel."

"But Your Grace would kill her!" cried the doctor.

"The French can do as they like," replied His Grace. "I do not know, no more do you, what would happen if this degrading instrument were employed, but what I do know is that a true English physician should cure his patients only with the old English remedies."

This physician, who was beginning to make a big reputation, lost all his practice in the great world. Another doctor was called in, who asked me some improper questions about Puff, and who informed me that the real device of the English was: *Dieu et mon droit congugal!*

One night I heard the voice of the French Cat in the street. Nobody could see us; I climbed up the chimney and, appearing on the housetop, cried, "In the rain-trough!" This response gave him wings; he was at my side in the twinkling of an eye. Would you believe that this French Cat had the audacity to take advantage of my exclamation. He cried, "Come to my arms," daring to become familiar with me, a Cat of distinction, without knowing me better. I regarded him frigidly and, to give him a lesson, I told him that I belonged to the Temperance Society.

"I see, sir," I said to him, "by your accent and by the looseness of your conversation, that you, like all Catholic Cats, are inclined to laugh and make sport, believing that confession will purge you, but in England we have another standard of morality. We are always respectable, even in our pleasures."

This young Cat, struck by the majesty of English cant, listened to me with a kind of attention which made me hope I could convert him to Protestantism. He then told me in purple words that he would do anything I wished provided I would permit him to adore me. I looked at him without being able to reply because his very beautiful and splendid eyes sparkled like stars; they lighted the night. Made bold by my silence, he cried "Dear Minette!"

"What new indecency is this?" I demanded, being well aware that French Cats are very free in their references.

Brisquet assured me that on the continent everybody, even the King himself, said to his daughter, *Ma petite Minette*, to show his affection, that many of the prettiest and most aristocratic young wives called their husbands, *Mon petit chat*, even when they did not love them. If I wanted to please him I would call him, *Mon petit homme!* Then he raised his paws with infinite grace. Thoroughly frightened I ran away. Brisquet was so happy that he sang *Rule Britannia*, and the next day his dear voice hummed again in my ears.

"Ah! you also are in love, dear Beauty," my mistress said to me, observing me extended on the carpet, the paws flat, the body in soft abandon, bathing in the poetry of my memories.

I was astonished that a woman should show so much intelligence, and so, raising my dorsal spine, I began to rub up against her legs and to purr lovingly with the deepest chords of my contralto voice.

While my mistress was scratching my head and caressing me and while I was looking at her tenderly a scene occurred in Bond Street which had terrible results for me.

Puck, a nephew of Puff's, in line to succeed him and who, for the time being, lived in the barracks of the Life Guards, ran into my dear Brisquet. The sly Captain Puck complimented the *attaché* on his success with me, adding that I had resisted the most charming Toms in England. Brisquet, foolish, vain Frenchman that he was, responded that he would be happy to gain my attention, but that he had a horror of Cats who spoke to him of temperance, the Bible, etc.

"Oh!" said Puck, "she talks to you then?"

Dear French Brisquet thus became a victim of English diplomacy, but later he committed one of these impardonable faults which irritate all well-bred Cats in England. This little idiot was truly very inconsistent. Did he not bow to me in Hyde Park and try to talk with me familiarly as if we were well acquainted? I looked straight through him coldly and severely. The coachman seeing this Frenchman insult me slashed him with his whip. Brisquet was cut but not killed and he received the blow with such nonchalance, continuing to look at me, that I was absolutely fascinated. I loved him for the manner in which he took his punishment, seeing only me, feeling only the favour of my presence, conquering the natural inclination of Cats to flee at the slightest warning of hostility. He could not know that I came near dying, in spite of my apparent coldness. From that moment I made up my mind to elope. That evening, on the roof, I threw myself tremblingly into his arms.

"My dear," I asked him, "have you the capital necessary to pay damages to old Puff?"

"I have no other capital," replied the French Cat, laughing, "than the hairs of my moustache, my four paws, and this tail." Then he swept the gutter with a proud gesture.

"Not any capital," I cried, "but then you are only an adventurer, my dear!"

"I love adventures," he said to me tenderly. "In France it is the custom to fight a duel in the circumstances to which you allude. French Cats have recourse to their claws and not to their gold."

"Poor country," I said to him, "and why does it send beasts so denuded of capital to the foreign embassies?"

"That's simple enough," said Brisquet. "Our new government does not love money — at least it does not love its employees to have money. It only seeks intellectual capacity."

Dear Brisquet answered me so lightly that I began to fear he was conceited.

"Love without money is nonsense," I said. "While you were seeking food you would not occupy yourself with me, my dear."

By way of response this charming Frenchman assured me that he was a direct descendant of Puss in Boots. Besides he had ninety-nine ways of borrowing money and we would have, he said, only a single way of spending it. To conclude, he knew music and could give lessons. In fact, he sang to me, in poignant tones, a national romance of his country, *Au clair de la lune*....

At this inopportune moment, when seduced by his reasoning, I had promised dear Brisquet to run away with him as soon as he could keep a wife comfortably, Puck appeared, followed by several other Cats.

"I am lost!" I cried.

The very next day, indeed, the bench of Doctors' Commons was occupied by a *procès-verbal* in criminal conversation. Puff was deaf; his nephews took advantage of his weakness. Questioned by them, Puff said that at night I had flattered him by calling him, *Mon petit homme!* This was one of the most terrible things against me, because I could not explain where I had learned these words of love. The judge, without knowing it, was prejudiced against me, and I noted that he was in his second childhood. His lordship never suspected the low intrigues of which I was the victim. Many little Cats, who should have defended me against public opinion, swore that Puff was always asking for his angel, the joy of his eyes, his sweet Beauty! My own mother, come to London, refused to see me or to speak to me, saying that an English Cat should always be above suspicion, and that I had embittered her old age. Finally the servants testified against me. I then saw perfectly clearly how everybody lost his head in England. When it is a matter of a criminal conversation, all sentiment is dead; a mother is no longer a mother, a nurse wants to take back her milk, and all the Cats howl in the streets. But the most infamous thing of all was that my old attorney who, in his time, would believe in the innocence of the Queen of England, to whom I had confessed everything to the last detail, who had assured me that there was no reason to whip a Cat, and to whom, to prove my innocence, I avowed that I did not even know the meaning of the words, "criminal conversation" (he told me that the crime was so called precisely because one spoke so little while committing it), this attorney, bribed by Captain Puck, defended me so badly that my case appeared to be lost. Under these circumstances I went on the stand myself.

"My Lords," I said, "I am an English Cat and I am innocent. What would be said of the justice of old England if...."

Hardly had I pronounced these words than I was interrupted by a murmur of voices, so strongly had the public been influenced by the *Cat-Chronicle* and by Puck's friends.

"She questions the justice of old England which has created the jury!" cried some one.

"She wishes to explain to you, My Lords," cried my adversary's abominable lawyer, "that she went on the rooftop with a French Cat in order to convert him to the Anglican faith, when, as a matter of fact, she went there to learn how to say, *Mon petit homme*, in French, to her husband, to listen to the abominable principles of papism, and to learn to disregard the laws and customs of old England!"

Such piffle always drives an English audience wild. Therefore the words of Puck's attorney were received with tumultuous applause. I was condemned at the age of twenty-six months, when I could prove that I still was ignorant of the very meaning of the word, Tom. But from all this I gathered that it was on account of such practices that Albion was called Old England.

I fell into a deep miscathropy which was caused less by my divorce than by the death of my dear Brisquet, whom Puck had had killed by a mob, fearing his vengeance. Also nothing made me more furious than to hear the loyalty of English Cats spoken of.

You see, O! French Animals, that in familiarizing ourselves with men, we borrow from them all their vices and bad institutions. Let us return to the wild life where we obey only our instincts, and where we do not find customs in conflict with the sacred wishes of Nature. At this moment I am writing a treatise on the abuse of the working classes of animals, in order to get them to pledge themselves to refrain from turning spits, to refuse to allow themselves to be harnessed to carriages, in order, to sum up, to teach them the means of protecting themselves against the oppression of the grand aristocracy. Although we are celebrated for our scribbling I believe that Miss Martineau would not repudiate me. You know that on the continent literature has become the haven of all Cats who protest against the immoral monopoly of marriage, who resist the tyranny of institutions, and who desire to encourage natural laws. I have omitted to tell you that, although Brisquet's body was slashed with a wound in the back, the coroner, by an infamous hypocrisy, declared that he had poisoned himself with arsenic, as if so gay, so light-headed a Cat could have reflected long enough on the subject of life to conceive so serious an idea, and as if a Cat whom I loved could have the least desire to quit this existence! But with Marsh's apparatus spots have been found on a plate.

Honoré de Balzac.

Translated by Carl Van Vechten.

GIPSY

On a fair Saturday afternoon in November Penrod's little old dog Duke returned to the ways of his youth and had trouble with a strange cat on the back porch. This indiscretion, so uncharacteristic, was due to the agitation of a surprised moment, for Duke's experience had inclined him to a peaceful pessimism, and he had no ambition for hazardous undertakings of any sort. He was given to musing but not to avoidable action, and he seemed habitually to hope for something which he was pretty sure would not happen. Even in his sleep, this gave him an air of wistfulness.

Thus, being asleep in a nook behind the metal refuse-can, when the strange cat ventured to ascend the steps of the porch, his appearance was so unwarlike that the cat felt encouraged to extend its field of reconnaissance — for the cook had been careless, and the backbone of a three-pound whitefish lay at the foot of the refuse-can.

This cat was, for a cat, needlessly tall, powerful, independent, and masculine. Once, long ago, he had been a roly-poly pepper-and-salt kitten; he had a home in those days, and a name, "Gipsy," which he abundantly justified. He was precocious in dissipation. Long before his adolescence, his lack of domesticity was ominous, and he had formed bad companionships. Meanwhile, he grew so rangy, and developed such length and power of leg and such traits of character, that the father of the little girl who owned him was almost convincing when he declared that the young cat was half broncho and half Malay pirate — though, in the light of Gipsy's later career, this seems bitterly unfair to even the lowest orders of bronchos and Malay pirates.

No; Gipsy was not the pet for a little girl. The rosy hearthstone and sheltered rug were too circumspect for him. Surrounded by the comforts of middle-class respectability, and profoundly oppressed, even in his youth, by the Puritan ideals of the household, he sometimes experienced a sense of suffocation. He wanted free air and he wanted free life; he wanted the lights, the lights, and the music. He abandoned the *bourgeoisie* irrevocably. He went forth in a May twilight, carrying the evening beefsteak with him, and joined the underworld.

His extraordinary size, his daring, and his utter lack of sympathy soon made him the leader — and, at the same time, the terror — of all the loose-lived cats in a wide neighbourhood. He contracted no friendships and had no confidants. He seldom slept in the same place twice in succession, and though he was wanted by the police, he was not found. In appearance he did not lack distinction of an ominous sort; the slow, rhythmic, perfectly controlled mechanism of his tail, as he impressively walked abroad, was incomparably sinister. This stately and dangerous walk of his, his long, vibrant whiskers, his scars, his yellow eye, so ice-cold, so fire-hot, haughty as the eye of Satan, gave him the deadly air of a mousquetaire duellist. His soul was in that walk and in that eye; it could be read — the soul of a bravo of fortune, living on his wits and his valour, asking no favours and granting no quarter. Intolerant, proud, sullen, yet watchful and constantly planning — purely a militarist, believing in slaughter as in a religion, and confident that art, science, poetry, and the good of the world were happily advanced thereby — Gipsy had become, though technically not a wildcat, undoubtedly the most untamed cat at large in the civilized world. Such, in brief, was the terrifying creature which now elongated its neck, and, over the top step of the porch, bent a calculating scrutiny upon the wistful and slumberous Duke.

The scrutiny was searching but not prolonged. Gipsy muttered contemptuously to himself, "Oh, sheol; I'm not afraid o' *that*!" And he approached the fishbone, his padded feet making no noise upon the boards. It was a desirable fishbone, large, with a considerable portion of the fish's tail still attached to it.

It was about a foot from Duke's nose, and the little dog's dreams began to be troubled by his olfactory nerve. This faithful sentinel, on guard even while Duke slept, signalled that alarums and excursions by parties unknown were taking place, and suggested that attention might well be paid. Duke opened one drowsy eye. What that eye beheld was monstrous.

Here was a strange experience — the horrific vision in the

midst of things so accustomed. Sunshine fell sweetly upon porch and backyard; yonder was the familiar stable, and from its interior came the busy hum of a carpenter shop, established that morning by Duke's young master, in association with Samuel Williams and Herman. Here, close by, were the quiet refuse-can and the wonted brooms and mops leaning against the latticed wall at the end of the porch, and there, by the foot of the steps, was the stone slab of the cistern, with the iron cover displaced and lying beside the round opening, where the carpenters had left it, not half an hour ago, after lowering a stick of wood into the water, "to season it." All about Duke were these usual and reassuring environs of his daily life, and yet it was his fate to behold, right in the midst of them, and in ghastly juxtaposition to his face, a thing of nightmare and lunacy.

Gipsy had seized the fishbone by the middle. Out from one side of his head, and mingling with his whiskers, projected the long, spiked spine of the big fish: down from the other side of that ferocious head dangled the fish's tail, and from above the remarkable effect thus produced shot the intolerable glare of two yellow eyes. To the gaze of Duke, still blurred by slumber, this monstrosity was all of one piece — the bone seemed a living part of it. What he saw was like those interesting insect-faces which the magnifying glass reveals to great M. Fabre. It was impossible for Duke to maintain the philosophic calm of M. Fabre, however; there was no magnifying glass between him and this spined and spiky face. Indeed, Duke was not in a position to think the matter over quietly. If he had been able to do that, he would have said to himself: "We have here an animal of most peculiar and unattractive appearance, though, upon examination, it seems to be only a cat stealing a fishbone. Nevertheless, as the thief is large beyond all my recollection of cats and has an unpleasant stare, I will leave this spot at once."

On the contrary, Duke was so electrified by his horrid awakening that he completely lost his presence of mind. In the very instant of his first eye's opening, the other eye and his mouth behaved similarly, the latter loosing upon the quiet air one shriek of mental agony before the little dog scrambled to his feet and gave further employment to his voice in a frenzy of profanity. At the same time the subterranean diapason of a demoniac bass viol was heard; it rose to a wail, and rose and rose again till it screamed like a small siren. It was Gipsy's war-cry, and, at the sound of it, Duke became a frothing maniac. He made a convulsive frontal attack upon the hobgoblin — and the massacre began.

Never releasing the fishbone for an instant, Gipsy laid back his ears in a chilling way, beginning to shrink into himself like a concertina, but rising amidships so high that he appeared to be giving an imitation of that peaceful beast, the dromedary. Such was not his purpose, however, for, having attained his greatest possible altitude, he partially sat down and elevated his right arm after the manner of a semaphore. This semaphore arm remained rigid for a second, threatening; then it vibrated with inconceivable rapidity, feinting. But it was the treacherous left that did the work. Seemingly this left gave Duke three lightning little pats upon the right ear, but the change in his voice indicated that these were no love-taps. He yelled "help!" and "bloody murder!"

Never had such a shattering uproar, all vocal, broken out upon a peaceful afternoon. Gipsy possessed a vocabulary for cat-swearing certainly second to none out of Italy, and probably equal to the best there, while Duke remembered and uttered things he had not thought of for years.

The hum of the carpenter shop ceased, and Sam Williams appeared in the stable doorway. He stared insanely.

"My gorry!" he shouted. "Duke's havin' a fight with the biggest cat you ever saw in your life! C'mon!"

His feet were already in motion toward the battlefield, with Penrod and Herman hurrying in his wake. Onward they sped, and Duke was encouraged by the sight and sound of these reinforcements to increase his own outrageous clamours and to press home his attack. But he was ill-advised. This time it was the right arm of the semaphore that dipped — and Duke's honest nose was but too conscious of what happened in consequence.

A lump of dirt struck the refuse-can with violence, and Gipsy beheld the advance of overwhelming forces. They rushed upon him from two directions, cutting off the steps of the porch. Undaunted, the formidable cat raked Duke's nose again, somewhat more lingeringly, and prepared to depart with his fishbone. He had little fear for himself, because he was inclined to think that, unhampered, he could whip anything on earth; still, things seemed to be growing rather warm and he saw nothing to prevent his leaving.

And though he could laugh in the face of so unequal an antagonist as Duke, Gipsy felt that he was never at his best or able to do himself full justice unless he could perform that feline operation inaccurately known as "spitting." To his notion, this was an absolute essential to combat; but, as all cats of the slightest pretensions to technique perfectly understand, it can neither be well done nor produce the best effects unless the mouth be opened to its utmost capacity so as to expose the beginnings of the alimentary canal, down which — at least that is the intention of the threat — the opposing party will soon be passing. And Gipsy could not open his mouth without relinquishing his fishbone.

Therefore, on small accounts he decided to leave the field to his enemies and to carry the fishbone elsewhere. He took two giant leaps. The first landed him upon the edge of the porch. There, without an instant's pause, he gathered his fur-sheathed muscles, concentrated himself into one big steel spring, and launched himself superbly into space. He made a stirring picture, however brief, as he left the solid porch behind him and sailed upward on an ascending curve into the sunlit air. His head was proudly up; he was the incarnation of menacing power and of self-confidence. It is possible that the white-fish's spinal column and flopping tail had interfered with his vision, and in launching himself he may have mistaken the dark, round opening of the cistern for its dark, round cover. In that case, it was a leap calculated and executed with precision, for as the boys clamoured their pleased astonishment, Gipsy descended accurately into the orifice and passed majestically from public view, with the fishbone still in his mouth and his haughty head still high.

There was a grand splash!

Booth Tarkington.

THE BLUE DRYAD

"According to that theory" — said a critical friend, *à propos* of the last story but one — "susceptibility of 'discipline' would be the chief test of animal character, which means that the best dogs get their character from men. If so — "

"You pity the poor brutes?"

"Oh no. I was going to say that on that principle cats should have next to no character at all."

"They have plenty," I said, "but it's usually bad — at least hopelessly unromantic. Who ever heard of a heroic or self-denying cat? Cats do what they like, not what you want them to do."

He laughed. "Sometimes they do what you like very much. You haven't heard Mrs. Warburton-Kinneir's cat-story?"

"The Warburton-Kinneirs! I didn't know they were back in England."

"Oh yes. They've been six months in Hampshire, and now they are in town. She has Thursday afternoons."

"Good," I said, "I'll go the very next Friday, and take my chance...."

Fortunately only one visitor appeared to tea. And as soon as I had explained my curiosity, he joined me in petitioning for the story which follows: —

*****

Stoffles was her name, a familiar abbreviation, and Mephistophelian was her nature. She had all the usual vices of the feline tribe, including a double portion of those which men are so fond of describing as feminine. Vain, indolent, selfish, with a highly cultivated taste for luxury and neatness in her personal appearance, she was distinguished by all those little irritating habits and traits for which nothing but an affectionate heart (a thing in her case conspicuous by its absence) can atone.

99

It would be incorrect, perhaps, to say that Stoffles did not care for the society of my husband and myself. She liked the best of everything, and these our circumstances allowed us to give her. For the rest, though in kitten days suspected of having caught a mouse, she had never been known in after life to do anything which the most lax of economists could describe as useful. She would lie all day in the best arm-chair enjoying real or pretended slumbers, which never affected her appetite at supper-time; although in that eventide which is the feline morn she would, if certain of a sufficient number of admiring spectators, condescend to amuse their dull human intelligence by exhibitions of her dexterity. But she was soon bored, and had no conception of altruistic effort. Abundantly cautious and prudent in all matters concerning her own safety and comfort, she had that feline celerity of vanishing like air or water before the foot, hand, or missile of irritated man; while on the other hand, when a sensitive specimen of the gentler sex (my grandmother, for example) was attentively holding the door open for her, she would stiffen and elongate her whole body, and, regardless of all exhibitions of kindly impatience, proceed out of the drawing-room as slowly as a funeral *cortège* of crocodiles.

A good-looking Persian cat is an ornamental piece of furniture in a house; but though fond of animals, I never succeeded in getting up an affection for Stoffles until the occurrence of the incident here to be related. Even in this, however, I cannot conceal from myself that the share which she took was taken, as usual, solely for her own satisfaction.

We lived, you know, in a comfortable old-fashioned house facing the highroad, on the slope of a green hill from which one looked across the gleaming estuary (or the broad mud-flats) of Southampton Water on to the rich, rolling woodland of the New Forest. I say we, but in fact for some months I had been alone, and my husband had just returned from one of his sporting and scientific expeditions in South America. He had already won fame as a naturalist, and had succeeded in bringing home alive quite a variety of beasts, usually of the reptile order, whose extreme rarity seemed to me a merciful provision of Nature.

But all his previous triumphs were completely eclipsed, I soon learned, by the capture, alive, on this last expedition, of an abominably poisonous snake, known to those who knew it as the Blue Dryad, or more familiarly in backwoods slang, as the Half-hour Striker, in vague reference to its malignant and fatal qualities. The time in which a snake-bite takes effect is, by the way, no very exact test of its virulence, the health and condition not only of the victim, but of the snake, having of course to be taken into account.

But the Blue Dryad, sometimes erroneously described as a variety of rattlesnake, is, I understand, supposed to kill the average man, under favourable circumstances, in less time even than the deadly Copperhead — which it somewhat resembles, except that it is larger in size, and bears a peculiar streak of faint peacock-blue down the back, only perceptible in a strong light. This precious reptile was destined for the Zoological Gardens.

Being in extremely delicate health at the time, I need hardly say that I knew nothing of these gruesome details until afterwards. Henry (that is my husband), after entering my room with a robust and sunburned appearance that did my heart good, merely observed — as soon as we had exchanged greetings — that he had brought home a pretty snake which "wouldn't (just as long, that is to say, as it couldn't) do the slightest harm," — an evasive assurance which I accepted as became the nervous wife of an enthusiastic naturalist. I believe I insisted on its not coming into the house.

The cook, indeed, on my husband expressing a wish to put it in the kitchen, had taken up a firmer position: she had threatened to "scream" if "the vermin" were introduced into her premises; which ultimatum, coming from a stalwart young woman with unimpaired lungs, was sufficient.

Fortunately the weather was very hot (being in July of the ever-memorable summer of 1893), so it was decided that the Blue Dryad, wrapped in flannel and securely confined in a basket, should be left in the sun, on the farthest corner of the verandah, during the hour or so in the afternoon when my husband had to visit the town on business.

He had gone off with a cousin of mine, an officer of Engineers in India, stationed, I think, at Lahore, and home on leave. I remember that they were a long time, or what seemed to me a long time, over their luncheon; and the last remark of our guest as he came out of the dining-room remained in my head as even meaningless words will run in the head of any idle invalid shut up for most of the day in a silent room. What he said was, in the positive tone of one emphasizing a curious and surprising statement, "D'you know, by the way, it's the *one* animal that doesn't care a rap for the cobra." And, my husband seeming to express disbelief and a desire to change the subject as they entered my boudoir, "It's a holy fact! Goes for it, so smart! Has the beggar on toast before you can say 'Jack Robinson!'"

The observation did not interest me, but simply ran in my head. Then they came into my room, only for a few moments, as I was not to be tired. The Engineer tried to amuse Stoffles, who was seized with such a fit of mortal boredom that he transferred his attentions to Ruby, the Gordon setter, a devoted and inseparable friend of mine, under whose charge I was shortly left as they passed out of the house. The Lieutenant, it appears, went last, and inadvertently closed without fastening the verandah door. Thereby hangs a tale of the most trying quarter of an hour it has been my lot to experience.

I suppose I may have been asleep for ten minutes or so when I was awakened by the noise of Ruby's heavy body jumping out through the open window. Feeling restless and seeing me asleep, he had imagined himself entitled to a short spell off guard. Had the door not been ostensibly latched he would have made his way out by it, being thoroughly used to opening doors and such tricks — a capacity which in fact proved fatal to him. That it was unlatched I saw in a few moments, for the dog on his return forced it open with a push and trotted up in a disturbed manner to my bedside. I noticed a tiny spot of blood on the black side of his nose, and naturally supposed he had scratched himself against a bush or a piece of wire. "Ruby," I said, "what have you been doing?" Then he whined as if in pain, crouching close to my side and shaking in every limb. I should say that I was myself lying with a shawl over my feet on a deep sofa with a high back. I turned to look at Stoffles, who was slowly perambulating the room, looking for flies and other insects (her favourite amusement) on the wainscot. When I glanced again at the dog his appearance filled me with horror; he was standing, obviously from pain, swaying from side to side and breathing hard. As I watched, his body grew more and more rigid. With his eyes fixed on the half-open door, he drew back as if from the approach of some dreaded object, raised his head with a pitiful attempt at a bark, which broke off into a stifled howl, rolled over sideways suddenly, and lay dead. The horrid stiffness of the body, almost resembling a stuffed creature overset, made me believe that he had died as he stood, close to my side, perhaps meaning to defend me — more probably, since few dogs would be proof against such a terror, trusting that I should protect him against the *thing coming in at the door*. Unable to resist the unintelligible idea that the dog had been frightened to death, I followed the direction of his last gaze, and at first saw nothing. The next moment I observed round the corner of the verandah door a small, dark, and slender object, swaying gently up and down like a dry bough in the wind. It had passed right into the room with the same slow, regular motion before I realized what it was and what had happened.

My poor, stupid Ruby must have nosed at the basket on the verandah till he succeeded somehow in opening it, and have been bitten in return for his pains by the abominable beast which had been warranted in this insufficient manner to do no harm, and which I now saw angrily rearing its head and hissing fiercely at the dead dog within three yards of my face.

I am not one of those women who jump on chairs or tables when they see a mouse, but I have a constitutional horror of the most harmless reptiles. Watching the Blue Dryad as it glided across the patch of sunlight streaming in from the open window, and knowing what it was, I confess to being as nearly frightened out of my wits as I ever hope to be. If I had been well, perhaps I might have managed to scream and run away. As it was, I simply dared not speak or move a finger for fear of attracting the beast's attention to myself. Thus I remained a terrified spectator of the astonishing scene which followed. The whole thing seemed to me like a dream. As the beast entered the room, I seemed again to hear my cousin making the remark above mentioned about the cobra. *What* animal, I wondered dreamily, could he have meant? Not Ruby! Ruby was dead. I looked at his stiff body again and shuddered. The whistle of a train sounded from the valley below, and then an errand-boy passed along the road at the back of the house (for the second or third time that day) singing in a cracked voice the fragment of a popular melody, of which I am sorry to say I know no more —

"I've got a little cat,
And I'm very fond of that;
But daddy wouldn't buy me a bow, wow, wow;"

the *wow-wows* becoming fainter and further as the youth strode down the hill. If I had been "myself," as the poor folk say, this coincidence would have made me laugh, for at that very moment Stoffles, weary of patting flies and spiders on the back, appeared gently purring on the crest, so to speak, of the sofa.

It has often occurred to me since that if the scale of things had been enlarged — if Stoffles, for example, had been a Bengal tiger, and the Dryad a boa-constrictor or crocodile, — the tragedy which followed would have been worthy of the pen of any sporting and dramatic historian. I can only say that, being transacted in such objectionable proximity to myself, the thing was as impressive as any combat of mastodon and iguanodon could have been to primitive man.

Stoffles, as I have said, was inordinately vain and self-conscious. Stalking along the top of the sofa-back and bearing erect the bushy banner of her magnificent tail, she looked the most ridiculous creature imaginable. She had proceeded half-way on this pilgrimage towards me when suddenly, with the rapidity of lightning, as her ear caught the sound of the hiss and her eyes fell upon the Blue Dryad, her whole civilized "play-acting" demeanour vanished, and her body stiffened and contracted to the form of a watchful wild beast with the ferocious and instinctive antipathy to a natural enemy blazing from its eyes. No change of a shaken kaleidoscope could have been more complete or more striking. In one light bound she was on the floor in a compressed, defensive attitude, with all four feet close together, near, but not too near, the unknown but clearly hostile intruder; and to my surprise, the snake turned and made off towards the window. Stoffles trotted lightly after, obviously interested in its method of locomotion. Then she made a long arm and playfully dropped a paw upon its tail. The snake wriggled free in a moment, and coiling its whole length, some three and a half feet, fronted this new and curious antagonist.

At the very first moment, I need hardly say, I expected that one short stroke of that little pointed head against the cat's delicate body would quickly have settled everything. But one is apt to forget that a snake (I suppose because in romances snakes always "dart") can move but slowly and awkwardly over a smooth surface, such as a tiled or wooden floor. The long body, in spite of its wonderful construction, and of the attitudes in which it is frequently drawn, is no less subject to the laws of gravitation than that of a hedgehog. A snake that "darts" when it has nothing secure to hold on by, only overbalances itself. With half or two-thirds of the body firmly coiled against some rough object or surface, the head — of a poisonous snake at least — is indeed a deadly weapon of precision. This particular reptile, perhaps by some instinct, had now wriggled itself on to a large and thick fur rug about twelve feet square, upon which arena took place the extraordinary contest that followed.

The audacity of the cat astonished me from the first. I have no reason to believe she had ever seen a snake before, yet by a sort of instinct she seemed to know exactly what she was doing. As the Dryad raised its head, with glittering eyes and forked tongue, Stoffles crouched with both front paws in the air, sparring as I had seen her do sometimes with a large moth. The first round passed so swiftly that mortal eye could hardly see with distinctness what happened. The snake made a dart, and the cat, all claws, aimed two rapid blows at its advancing head. The first missed, but the second I could see came home, as the brute, shaking its neck and head, withdrew further into the jungle — I mean, of course, the rug. But Stoffles, who had no idea of the match ending in this manner, crept after it, with an air of attractive carelessness which was instantly rewarded. A full two feet of the Dryad's body straightened like a black arrow, and seemed to strike right into the furry side of its antagonist — seemed, I say, to slow going human eyes; but the latter shrank, literally *fell* back, collapsing with such suddenness that she seemed to have turned herself inside out, and become the mere skin of a cat. As the serpent recovered itself, she pounced on it like lightning, driving at least half a dozen claws well home, and then, apparently realizing that she had not a good enough hold, sprang lightly into the air from off the body, alighting about a yard off. There followed a minute of sparring in the air; the snake seemingly half afraid to strike, the cat waiting on its every movement.

Now, the poisonous snake when provoked is an irritable animal, and the next attack of the Dryad, maddened by the scratchings of puss and its own unsuccessful exertions, was so furious, and so close to myself, that I shuddered for the result. Before this stage, I might perhaps, with a little effort have escaped, but now panic fear glued me to the spot; indeed I could not have left my position on the sofa without almost treading upon Stoffles, whose bristling back was not a yard from my feet. At last, I thought — as the Blue Dryad, for one second coiled close as a black silk cable, sprang out the next as straight and sharp as the piston-rod of an engine, — this lump of feline vanity and conceit is done for, and — I could not help thinking — it will probably be my turn next! Little did I appreciate the resources of Stoffles, who without a change in her vigilant pose, without a wink of her fierce green eyes, sprang backwards and upwards on to the top of me and there confronted the enemy as calm as ever, sitting, if you please, upon my feet! I don't know that any gymnastic performance ever surprised me more than this, though I have seen this very beast drop twenty feet from a window-sill on to a stone pavement without appearing to notice any particular change of level. Cats with so much plumage have probably their own reasons for not flying.

Trembling all over with fright, I could not but observe that she was trembling too — with rage. Whether instinct inspired her with the advantages of a situation so extremely unpleasant to me, I cannot say. The last act of the drama rapidly approached, and no more strategic catastrophe was ever seen.

For a snake, as everybody knows, naturally rears its head when fighting. In that position, though one may hit it with a stick, it is extremely difficult, as this battle had shown, to get hold of. Now, as the Dryad, curled to a capital S, quivering and hissing advanced for the last time to the charge, it was bound to strike across the edge of the sofa on which I lay, at the erect head of Stoffles, which vanished with a juggling celerity that would have dislocated the collar-bone of any other animal in creation. From such an exertion the snake recovered itself with an obvious effort, quick beyond question, but not nearly quick enough. Before I could well see that it had missed its aim, Stoffles had launched out like a spring released, and, burying eight or ten claws in the back of its enemy's head, pinned it down against the stiff cushion of the sofa. The tail of the agonized reptile flung wildly in the air and flapped on the arched back of the imperturbable tigress. The whiskered muzzle of Stoffles dropped quietly, and her teeth met once, twice, thrice, like the needle and hook of a sewing-machine, in the neck of the Blue Dryad; and when, after much deliberation, she let it go, the beast fell into a limp tangle on the floor.

When I saw that the thing was really dead I believe I must have fainted. Coming to myself, I heard hurried steps and voices. "Great heavens!" my husband was screaming, "where has the brute got to?" "It's all right," said the Engineer; "just you come and look here, old man. Commend me to the coolness of that cat. After the murder of your priceless specimen, here's Stoffles cleaning her fur in one of her serenest Anglo-Saxon attitudes."

So she was. My husband looked grave as I described the scene. "Didn't I tell you so?" said the Engineer, "and this beast, I take it, is worse than any cobra."

I can easily believe he was right. From the gland of the said beast, as I afterwards learned, they extracted enough poison to be the death of twenty full-grown human beings.

Tightly clasped between its minute teeth was found (what interested me more) a few long hairs, late the property of Stoffles.

Stoffles, however — she is still with us — has a superfluity of long hair, and is constantly leaving it about.

G. H. Powell.

DICK BAKER'S CAT

One of my comrades there — another of those victims of eighteen years of unrequited toil and blighted hopes — was one of the gentlest spirits that ever bore its patient cross in a weary exile: grave and simple Dick Baker, pocket-miner of Dead-Horse Gulch. He was forty-six, grey as a rat, earnest, thoughtful, slenderly educated, slouchily dressed and clay-soiled, but his heart was finer metal than any gold his shovel ever brought to light — than any, indeed, that ever was mined or minted.

Whenever he was out of luck and a little downhearted, he would fall to mourning over the loss of a wonderful cat he used to own (for where women and children are not, men of kindly impulses take up with pets, for they must love something). And he always spoke of the strange sagacity of that cat with the air of a man who believed in his secret heart that there was something human about it — maybe even supernatural.

I heard him talking about this animal once. He said:

"Gentlemen, I used to have a cat here, by the name of Tom Quartz, which you'd 'a' took an interest in, I reckon — , most anybody would. I had him here eight year — and he was the re-markablest cat I ever see. He was a large grey one of the Tom specie, an' he had more hard, natchral sense than any man in this camp — 'n a *power* of dignity — he wouldn't let the Gov'ner of Californy be familiar with him. He never ketched a rat in his life — 'peared to be above it. He never cared for nothing but mining. He knowed more about mining, that cat did, than any man I ever, ever see. You couldn't tell *him* noth'n' 'bout placer-diggin's — 'n as for pocket-mining, why he was just born for it. He would dig out after me an' Jim when we went over the hills prospect'n', and he would trot along behind us for as much as five mile, if we went so fur. An' he had the best judgment about mining-ground — why you never see anything like it. When we went to work, he'd scatter a glance around, 'n' if he didn't think much of the indications, he would give a look as much as to say, 'Well, I'll have to get you to excuse *me*,' 'n' without another word he'd hyste his nose into the air 'n' shove for home. But if the ground suited him, he would lay low 'n' keep dark till the first pan was washed, 'n' then he would sidle up 'n' take a look, an' if there was about six or seven grains of gold *he* was satisfied — he didn't want no better prospect 'n' that — 'n' then he would lay down on our coats and snore like a steamboat till we'd struck the pocket, an' then get up 'n' superintend. He was nearly lightnin' on superintending.

"Well, by an' by, up comes this yer quartz excitement. Everybody was into it — everybody was pick'n' 'n' blast'n' instead of shovelin' dirt on the hillside — everybody was putt'n' down a shaft instead of scrapin' the surface. Noth'n' would do Jim, but *we* must tackle the ledges, too, 'n' so we did. We commenced putt'n' down a shaft, 'n' Tom Quartz he begin to wonder what in the Dickens it was all about. *He* hadn't ever seen any mining like that before, 'n' he was all upset, as you may say — he couldn't come to a right understanding of it no way — it was too many for *him*. He was down on it too, you bet you — he was down on it powerful — 'n' always appeared to consider it the cussedest foolishness out. But that cat, you know, was *always* agin new-fangled arrangements — somehow he never could abide 'em. *You* know how it is with old habits. But by an' by Tom Quartz begin to git sort of reconciled a little, though he never *could* altogether understand that eternal sinkin' of a shaft an' never pannin' out anything. At last he got to comin' down in the shaft, hisself, to try to cipher it out. An' when he'd git the blues, 'n' feel kind o' scruffy, 'n' aggravated 'n' disgusted — knowin' as he did, that the bills was runnin' up all the time an' we warn't makin' a cent — he would curl up on a gunny-sack in the corner an' go to sleep. Well, one day when the shaft was down about eight foot, the rock got so hard that we had to put in a blast — the first blast'n' we'd ever done since Tom Quartz was born. An' then we lit the fuse 'n' clumb out 'n' got off 'bout fifty yards — 'n' forgot 'n' left Tom Quartz sound asleep on the gunny-sack. In 'bout a minute we seen a puff of smoke bust up out of the hole, 'n' then everything let go with an awful crash, 'n' about four million ton of rocks 'n' dirt 'n' smoke 'n' splinters shot up 'bout a mile an' a half into the air, an' by George, right in the dead centre of it was old Tom Quartz a-goin' end over end, an' a-snortin' an' a-sneez'n, an' a-clawin' an' a-reach'n' for things like all possessed. But it warn't no use, you know, it warn't no use. An' that was the last we see of *him* for about two minutes 'n' a half, an' then all of a sudden it begin to rain rocks and rubbage an' directly he come down ker-whoop about ten foot off f'm where we stood. Well, I reckon he was p'raps the orneriest-lookin' beast you ever see. One ear was sot back on his neck, 'n' his tail was stove up, 'n' his eye-winkers was singed off, 'n' he was all blacked up with powder an' smoke, an' all sloppy with mud 'n' slush f'm one end to the other. Well, sir, it warn't no use to try to apologize — we couldn't say a word. He took a sort of a disgusted look at hisself, 'n' then he looked at us — an' it was just exactly the same as if he had said — 'Gents, maybe *you* think it's smart to take advantage of a cat that ain't had no experience of quartz-minin', but *I* think *different*' — an' then he turned on his heel 'n' marched off home without ever saying another word.

"That was jest his style. An' maybe you won't believe it, but after that you never see a cat so prejudiced agin quartz-mining as what he was. An' by an' by when he *did* get to goin' down in the shaft ag'in, you'd 'a' been astonished at his sagacity. The minute we'd tetch off a blast 'n' the fuse'd begin to sizzle, he'd give a look as much as to say, 'Well, I'll have to git you to excuse *me*,' an' it was supris'n' the way he'd shin out of that hole 'n' go f'r a tree. Sagacity? It ain't no name for it. 'Twas *inspiration*!"

I said, "Well, Mr. Baker, his prejudice against quartz-mining *was* remarkable, considering how he came by it. Couldn't you ever cure him of it?"

"*Cure him!* No! When Tom Quartz was sot once, he was *always* sot — and you might 'a' blowed him up as much as three million times 'n' you'd never 'a' broken him of his cussed prejudice ag'in quartz-mining."

Mark Twain.

THE BLACK CAT

For the most wild, yet most homely narrative which I am about to pen, I neither expect nor solicit belief. Mad indeed would I be to expect it in a case where my very senses reject their own evidence. Yet mad am I not — and very surely do I not dream. But tomorrow I die, and today I would unburthen my soul. My immediate purpose is to place before the world plainly, succinctly, and without comment, a series of mere household events. In their consequences these events have terrified — have tortured — have destroyed me. Yet I will not attempt to expound them. To me they presented little but horror — to many they will seem less terrible than *baroques*. Hereafter, perhaps, some intellect may be found which will reduce my phantasm to the commonplace — some intellect more calm, more logical, and far less excitable than my own, which will perceive, in the circumstances I detail with awe, nothing more than an ordinary succession of very natural causes and effects.

From my infancy I was noted for the docility and humanity of my disposition. My tenderness of heart was even so conspicuous as to make me the jest of my companions. I was especially fond of animals, and was indulged by my parents with a great variety of pets. With these I spent most of my time, and never was so happy as when feeding and caressing them. This peculiarity of character grew with my growth, and in my manhood I derived from it one of my principal sources of pleasure. To those who have cherished an affection for a faithful and sagacious dog, I need hardly be at the trouble of explaining the nature or the intensity of the gratification thus derivable. There is something in the unselfish and self-sacrificing love of a brute which goes directly to the heart of him who has had frequent occasion to test the paltry friendship and gossamer fidelity of mere *Man*.

I married early, and was happy to find in my wife a disposition not uncongenial with my own. Observing my partiality for domestic pets, she lost no opportunity of procuring those of the most agreeable kind. We had birds, gold-fish, a fine dog, rabbits, a small monkey, and *a cat*.

This latter was a remarkably large and beautiful animal, entirely black, and sagacious to an astonishing degree. In speaking of his intelligence, my wife, who at heart was not a little tinctured with superstition, made frequent allusion to the ancient popular notion which regarded all black cats as witches in disguise. Not that she was ever *serious* upon this point, and I mention the matter at all for no better reason than that it happens just now to be remembered.

Pluto — this was the cat's name — was my favourite pet and playmate. I alone fed him, and he attended me wherever I went about the house. It was even with difficulty that I could prevent him from following me through the streets.

Our friendship lasted in this manner for several years, during which my general temperament and character — through the instrumentality of the Fiend Intemperance — had (I blush to confess it) experienced a radical alteration for the worse. I grew, day by day, more moody, more irritable, more regardless of the feelings of others. I suffered myself to use intemperate language to my wife. At length, I even offered her personal violence. My pets of course were made to feel the change in my disposition. I not only neglected but ill-used them. For Pluto, however, I still retained sufficient regard to restrain me from maltreating him, as I made no scruple of maltreating the rabbits, the monkey, or even the dog, when by accident, or through affection, they came in my way. But my disease grew upon me — for what disease is like Alcohol! — and at length even Pluto, who was now becoming old, and consequently somewhat peevish — even Pluto began to experience the effects of my ill-temper.

One night, returning home much intoxicated from one of my haunts about town, I fancied that the cat avoided my presence. I seized him, when, in his fright at my violence, he inflicted a slight wound upon my hand with his teeth. The fury of a demon instantly possessed me. I knew myself no longer. My original soul seemed at once to take its flight from my body, and a more than fiendish malevolence, gin-nurtured, thrilled every fiber of my frame. I took from my waistcoat-pocket a penknife, opened it, grasped the poor beast by the throat, and deliberately cut one of its eyes from the socket! I blush, I burn, I shudder, while I pen the damnable atrocity.

When reason returned with the morning — when I had slept off the fumes of the night's debauch — I experienced a sentiment half of horror, half of remorse, for the crime of which I had been guilty, but it was at best a feeble and equivocal feeling, and the soul remained untouched. I again plunged into excess, and soon drowned in wine all memory of the deed.

In the meantime the cat slowly recovered. The socket of the lost eye presented, it is true, a frightful appearance, but he no longer appeared to suffer any pain. He went about the house as usual, but, as might be expected, fled in extreme terror at my approach. I had so much of my old heart left as to be at first grieved by this evident dislike on the part of a creature which had once so loved me. But this feeling soon gave place to irritation. And then came, as if to my final and irrevocable overthrow, the spirit of Perverseness. Of this spirit philosophy takes no account. Yet I am not more sure that my soul lives than I am that per- verseness is one of the primitive impulses of the human heart — one of the indivisible primary faculties or sentiments which gave direction to the character of Man. Who has not, a hundred times, found himself committing a vile or a silly action for no other rea- son than because he knows he should *not*? Have we not a perpet- ual inclination, in the teeth of our best judgment, to violate that which is *Law*, merely because we understand it to be such? This spirit of perverseness, I say, came to my final overthrow. It was this unfathomable longing of the soul to *vex itself* — to offer vio- lence to its own nature — to do wrong for the wrong's sake only — that urged me to continue and finally to consummate the in- jury I had inflicted upon the unoffending brute. One morning, in cool blood, I slipped a noose about its neck and hung it to the limb of a tree; hung it with the tears streaming from my eyes, and with the bitterest remorse at my heart; hung it *because* I knew it had loved me, and *because* I felt it had given me no reason of of- fence; hung it *because* I knew that in so doing I was committing a sin — a deadly sin that would so jeopardize my immortal soul as to place it, if such a thing were possible, even beyond the reach of the infinite mercy of the Most Merciful and Most Terrible God.

On the night of the day on which this cruel deed was done, I was aroused from sleep by the cry of fire. The curtains of my bed were in flames. The whole house was blazing. It was with great difficulty that my wife, a servant, and myself, made our escape from the conflagration. The destruction was complete. My entire worldly wealth was swallowed up, and I resigned myself forward to despair.

I am above the weakness of seeking to establish a sequence of cause and effect between the disaster and the atrocity. But I am detailing a chain of facts, and wish not to leave even a possible link imperfect. On the day succeeding the fire, I visited the ruins. The walls with one exception had fallen in. This exception was found in a compartment wall, not very thick, which stood about the middle of the house, and against which had rested the head of my bed. The plastering had here in great measure resisted the action of the fire, a fact which I attributed to its having recently spread. About this wall a dense crowd were collected, and many persons seemed to be examining a particular portion of it with very minute and eager attention. The words "Strange!" "Singular!" and other similar expressions, excited my curiosity. I approached and saw, as if graven in *bas relief* upon the white surface the figure of a gigantic *cat*. The impression was given with an accuracy truly marvellous. There was a rope about the animal's neck.

When I first beheld this apparition — for I could scarcely regard it as less — my wonder and my terror were extreme. But at length reflection came to my aid. The cat, I remembered, had been hung in a garden adjacent to the house. Upon the alarm of fire this garden had been immediately filled by the crowd, by some one of whom the animal must have been cut from the tree and thrown through an open window into my chamber. This had probably been with the view of arousing me from sleep. The falling of other walls had compressed the victim of my cruelty into the substance of the freshly-spread plaster; the lime of which, with the flames and the *ammonia* from the carcass, had then accomplished the portraiture as I saw it.

Although I thus readily accounted to my reason, if not altogether to my conscience, for the startling fact just detailed, it did not the less fail to make a deep impression upon my fancy. For months I could not rid myself of the phantasm of the cat, and during this period there came back into my spirit a half-sentiment that seemed, but was not, remorse. I went so far as to regret the loss of the animal, and to look about me among the vile haunts which I now habitually frequented for another pet of the same species, and of somewhat similar appearance, with which to supply its place.

One night, as I sat half-stupefied in a den of more than infamy, my attention was suddenly drawn to some black object, reposing upon the head of one of the immense hogsheads of gin or of rum, which constituted the chief furniture of the apartment. I had been looking steadily at the top of this hogshead for some minutes, and what now caused me surprise was the fact that I had not sooner perceived the object thereupon. I approached it, and touched it with my hand. It was a black cat — a very large one — fully as large as Pluto, and closely resembling him in every respect but one. Pluto had not a white hair upon any portion of his body; but this cat had a large, although indefinite splotch of white, covering nearly the whole region of the breast.

Upon my touching him he immediately arose, purred loudly, rubbed against my hand, and appeared delighted with my notice. This, then, was the very creature of which I was in search. I at once offered to purchase it of the landlord; but this person made no claim to it — knew nothing of it — had never seen it before.

I continued my caresses, and when I prepared to go home the animal evinced a disposition to accompany me. I permitted it to do so, occasionally stooping and patting it as I proceeded. When it reached the house it domesticated itself at once, and became immediately a great favourite with my wife.

For my own part, I soon found a dislike to it arising within me. This was just the reverse of what I had anticipated, but — I know not how or why it was — its evident fondness for myself rather disgusted and annoyed. By slow degrees these feelings of disgust and annoyance rose into the bitterness of hatred. I avoided the creature; a certain sense of shame, and the remembrance of my former deed of cruelty, preventing me from physically abusing it. I did not, for some weeks, strike or otherwise violently ill-use it, but gradually — very gradually — I came to look upon it with unutterable loathing, and to flee silently from its odious presence as from the breath of a pestilence.

What added, no doubt, to my hatred of the beast was the discovery, on the morning after I brought it home, that, like Pluto, it also had been deprived of one of its eyes. This circumstance, however, only endeared it to my wife, who, as I have already said, possessed in a high degree that humanity of feeling which had once been my distinguishing trait, and the source of my simplest and purest pleasures.

With my aversion to this cat, however, its partiality for myself seemed to increase. It followed my footsteps with a pertinacity which it would be difficult to make the reader comprehend. Whenever I sat, it would crouch beneath my chair or spring upon my knees, covering me with its loathsome caresses. If I arose to walk it would get between my feet and thus nearly throw me down, or, fastening its long and sharp claws in my dress, clamber in this manner to my breast. At such times, although I longed to destroy it with a blow, I was yet withheld from so doing, partly by a memory of my former crime, but chiefly — let me confess it at once — by absolute *dread* of the beast.

This dread was not exactly a dread of physical evil — and yet I should be at a loss how otherwise to define it. I am almost ashamed to own — yes, even in this felon's cell, I am almost ashamed to own — that the terror and horror with which the animal inspired me had been heightened by one of the merest chimeras it would be possible to conceive. My wife had called my attention more than once to the character of the mark of white hair, of which I have spoken, and which constituted the sole visible difference between the strange beast and the one I had destroyed. The reader will remember that this mark, although large, had been originally very indefinite, but by slow degrees — degrees nearly imperceptible, and which for a long time my reason struggled to reject as fanciful — it had at length assumed a rigorous distinctness of outline. It was now the representation of an object that I shudder to name — and for this above all I loathed and dreaded, and would have rid myself of the monster *had I dared* — it was now, I say, the image of a hideous — of a ghastly thing — of the Gallows! — O, mournful and terrible engine of horror and of crime — of agony and of death!

And now was I indeed wretched beyond the wretchedness of mere humanity. And *a brute beast* — whose fellow I had contemptuously destroyed — *a brute beast* to work out for *me* — for me a man, fashioned in the image of the High God — so much of insufferable woe! Alas! neither by day nor by night knew I the blessing of rest any more! During the former the creature left me no moment alone; and in the latter I started hourly from dreams of unutterable fear, to find the hot breath of *the thing* upon my face, and its vast weight — an incarnate nightmare that I had no power to shake off — incumbent eternally upon my *heart!*

Beneath the pressure of torments such as these, the feeble remnant of the good within me succumbed. Evil thoughts became my sole intimates — the darkest and most evil of thoughts. The moodiness of my usual temper increased to hatred of all things and of all mankind; while from the sudden frequent and ungovernable outbursts of a fury to which I now blindly abandoned myself, my uncomplaining wife, alas! was the most usual and the most patient of sufferers.

One day she accompanied me upon some household errand into the cellar of the old building which our poverty compelled us to inhabit. The cat followed me down the steep stairs, and nearly throwing me headlong, exasperated me to madness. Uplifting an ax, and forgetting in my wrath the childish dread which had hitherto stayed my hand, I aimed a blow at the animal, which of course would have proved instantly fatal had it descended as I wished. But this blow was arrested by the hand of my wife. Goaded by the interference into a rage more than demoniacal, I withdrew my arm from her grasp and buried the ax in her brain. She fell dead upon the spot without a groan.

This hideous murder accomplished, I set myself forthwith and with entire deliberation to the task of concealing the body. I knew that I could not remove it from the house, either by day or by night, without the risk of being observed by the neighbours. Many projects entered my mind. At one period I thought of cutting the corpse into minute fragments and destroying them by fire. At another I resolved to dig a grave for it in the floor of the cellar. Again, I deliberated about casting it in the well in the yard — about packing it in a box, as if merchandise, with the usual arrangements, and so getting a porter to take it from the house. Finally I hit upon what I considered a far better expedient than either of these. I determined to wall it up in the cellar — as the monks of the middle ages are recorded to have walled up their victims.

For a purpose such as this the cellar was well adapted. Its walls were loosely constructed and had lately been plastered throughout with a rough plaster, which the dampness of the atmosphere had prevented from hardening. Moreover, in one of the walls was a projection caused by a false chimney or fireplace, that had been filled up and made to resemble the rest of the cellar. I made no doubt that I could readily displace the bricks at this point, insert the corpse, and wall the whole up as before, so that no eye could detect anything suspicious.

And in this calculation I was not deceived. By means of a crowbar I easily dislodged the bricks, and having carefully deposited the body against the inner wall, I propped it in that position, while with little trouble I relaid the whole structure as it originally stood. Having procured mortar, sand, and hair with every possible precaution, I prepared a plaster which could not be distinguished from the old, and with this I very carefully went over the new brick-work. When I had finished I felt satisfied that all was all right. The wall did not present the slightest appearance of having been disturbed. The rubbish on the floor was picked up with the minutest care. I looked around triumphantly, and said to myself — "Here at last, then, my labour has not been in vain."

My next step was to look for the beast which had been the cause of so much wretchedness, for I had at length firmly resolved to put it to death. Had I been able to meet with it at the moment there could have been no doubt of its fate, but it appeared that the crafty animal had been alarmed at the violence of my previous anger, and forbore to present itself in my present mood. It is impossible to describe or to imagine the deep, the blissful sense of relief which the absence of the detested creature occasioned in my bosom. It did not make its appearance during the night — and thus for one night at least since its introduction into the house I soundly and tranquilly slept, aye, *slept* even with the burden of murder upon my soul!

The second and the third day passed, and still my tormentor came not. Once again I breathed as a freeman. The monster, in terror, had fled the premises forever! I should behold it no more! My happiness was supreme! The guilt of my dark deed disturbed me but little. Some few inquiries had been made, but these had been readily answered. Even a search had been instituted — but of course nothing was to be discovered. I looked upon my future felicity as secured.

Upon the fourth day of the assassination, a party of the police came very unexpectedly into the house, and proceeded again to make rigorous investigation of the premises. Secure, however, in the inscrutability of my place of concealment, I felt no embarrassment whatever. The officers bade me accompany them in their search. They left no nook or corner unexplored. At length, for the third or fourth time they descended into the cellar. I quivered not in a muscle. My heart beat calmly as that of one who slumbers in innocence. I walked the cellar from end to end. I folded my arms upon my bosom, and roamed easily to and fro. The police were thoroughly satisfied, and prepared to depart. The glee at my heart was too strong to be restrained. I burned to say if but one word by way of triumph, and to render doubly sure their assurance of my guiltlessness.

"Gentlemen," I said at last, as the party ascended the steps, "I delight to have allayed your suspicions. I wish you all health, and a little more courtesy. By the by, gentlemen, this — this is a very well-constructed house," (In the rabid desire to say something easily, I scarcely knew what I uttered at all,) "I may say an *excel-*

lently well-constructed house. These walls — are you going, gentlemen? — these walls are solidly put together;" and here, through the mere frenzy of bravado, I rapped heavily with a cane which I held in my hand upon that very portion of the brick-work behind which stood the corpse of the wife of my bosom.

But may God shield and deliver me from the fangs of the arch-fiend! No sooner had the reverberation of my blows sunk into silence than I was answered by a voice from within the tomb! — by a cry, at first muffled and broken, like the sobbing of a child, and then quickly swelling into one long, loud, and continuous scream, utterly anomalous and inhuman — a howl — a wailing shriek, half of horror and half of triumph, such as might have arisen only out of hell, conjointly from the throats of the damned in their agony and of the demons that exult in the damnation.

Of my own thoughts it is folly to speak. Swooning, I staggered to the opposite wall. For one instant the party upon the stairs remained motionless, through extremity of terror and of awe. In the next a dozen stout arms were toiling at the wall. It fell bodily. The corpse, already greatly decayed and clotted with gore, stood erect before the eyes of the spectators. Upon its head, with red extended mouth and solitary eye of fire, sat the hideous beast whose craft had seduced me into murder, and whose informing voice had consigned me to the hangman. I had walled the monster up within the tomb.

Edgar Allan Poe.

MADAME JOLICŒUR'S CAT

Being somewhat of an age, and a widow of dignity — the late Monsieur Jolicœur has held the responsible position under Government of Ingénieur des Ponts et Chaussées — yet being also of a provocatively fresh plumpness, and a Marseillaise, it was of necessity that Madame Veuve Jolicœur, on being left lonely in the world save for the companionship of her adored Shah de Perse, should entertain expectations of the future that were antipodal and antagonistic: on the one hand, of an austere life suitable to a widow of a reasonable maturity and of an assured position; on the other hand, of a life, not austere, suitable to a widow still of a provocatively fresh plumpness and by birth a Marseillaise.

Had Madame Jolicœur possessed a severe temperament and a resolute mind — possessions inherently improbable, in view of her birthplace — she would have made her choice between these equally possible futures with a promptness and with a finality that would have left nothing at loose ends. So endowed, she would have emphasized her not excessive age by a slightly excessive gravity of dress and of deportment; and would have adorned it, and her dignified widowhood, by becoming dévote: and thereafter, clinging with a modest ostentation only to her piety, would have radiated, as time made its marches, an always increasingly exemplary grace. But as Madame Jolicœur did not possess a temperament that even bordered on severity, and as her mind was a sort that made itself up in at least twenty different directions in a single moment — as she was, in short, an entirely typical and therefore an entirely delightful Provençale — the situation was so much too much for her that, by the process of formulating a great variety of irreconcilable conclusions, she left everything at loose ends by not making any choice at all.

In effect, she simply stood attendant upon what the future had in store for her: and meanwhile avowedly clung only, in default of piety, to her adored Shah de Perse — to whom was given, as she declared in disconsolate negligence of her still provocatively fresh plumpness, all of the bestowable affection that remained in the devastated recesses of her withered heart.

To preclude any possibility of compromising misunderstanding, it is but just to Madame Jolicœur to explain at once that the personage thus in receipt of the contingent remainder of her blighted affections — far from being, as his name would suggest, an Oriental potentate temporarily domiciled in Marseille to whom she had taken something more than a passing fancy — was a Persian superb black cat; and a cat of such rare excellencies of character and of acquirements as fully to deserve all of the affection that any heart of the right sort — withered, or otherwise — was disposed to bestow upon him.

Cats of his perfect beauty, of his perfect grace, possibly might be found, Madame Jolicœur grudgingly admitted, in the Persian royal catteries; but nowhere else in the Orient, and nowhere at all in the Occident, she declared with an energetic conviction, possibly could there be found a cat who even approached him in intellectual development, in wealth of interesting accomplishments, and, above all, in natural sweetness of disposition — a sweetness so marked that even under extreme provocation he never had been known to thrust out an angry paw. This is not to say that the Shah de Perse was a characterless cat, a lymphatic nonentity. On occasion — usually in connection with food that was distasteful to him — he could have his resentments; but they were manifested always with a dignified restraint. His nearest approach to ill-mannered abruptness was to bat with a contemptuous paw the offending morsel from his plate; which brusque act he followed by fixing upon the bestower of unworthy food a coldly, but always politely, contemptuous stare. Ordinarily, however, his displeasure — in the matter of unsuitable food, or in other matters — was exhibited by no more overt action than his retirement to a corner — he had his choices in corners, governed by the intensity of his feelings — and there seating himself with his back turned scornfully to an offending world. Even in his kindliest corner, on such occasions, the expression of his scornful back was as a whole volume of wingéd words!

But the rare little cat tantrums of the Shah de Perse — if to his so gentle excesses may be applied so strong a term — were but as sun-spots on the effulgence of his otherwise constant amiability. His regnant desires, by which his worthy little life was governed, were to love and to please. He was the most cuddlesome cat, Madame Jolicœur unhesitatingly asserted, that ever had lived; and he had a purr — softly thunderous and winningly affectionate — that was in keeping with his cuddlesome ways. When, of his own volition, he would jump into her abundant lap and go to burrowing with his little soft round head beneath her soft round elbows, the while gurglingly purring forth his love for her, Madame Jolicœur, quite justifiably, at times was moved to tears. Equally was his sweet nature exhibited in his always eager willingness to show off his little train of cat accomplishments. He would give his paw with a courteous grace to any lady or gentleman — he drew the caste line rigidly — who asked for it. For his mistress, he would spring to a considerable height and clutch with his two soft paws — never by any mistake scratching — her outstretched wrist, and so would remain suspended while he delicately nibbled from between her fingers her edible offering. For her, he would make an almost painfully real pretence of being a dead cat: extending himself upon the rug with an exaggeratedly death-like rigidity — and so remaining until her command to be alive again brought him briskly to rub himself, rising on his hind legs and purring mellowly, against her comfortable knees.

All of these interesting tricks, with various others that may be passed over, he would perform with a lively zest whenever set at them by a mere word of prompting; but his most notable trick was a game in which he engaged with his mistress not at word of command, but — such was his intelligence — simply upon her setting the signal for it. The signal was a close-fitting white cap — to be quite frank, a night-cap — that she tied upon her head when it was desired that the game should be played.

It was of the game that Madame Jolicœur should assume her cap with an air of detachment and aloofness: as though no such entity as the Shah de Perse existed, and with an insisted-upon disregard of the fact that he was watching her alertly with his great golden eyes. Equally was it of the game that the Shah de Perse should affect — save for his alert watching — a like disregard of the doings of Madame Jolicœur: usually by an ostentatious pretence of washing his upraised hind leg, or by a like pretence of scrubbing his ears. These conventions duly having been observed, Madame Jolicœur would seat herself in her especial easy-chair, above the relatively high back of which her night-capped head a little rose. Being so seated, always with the air of aloofness and detachment, she would take a book from the table and make a show of becoming absorbed in its contents. Matters being thus advanced, the Shah de Perse would make a show of becoming absorbed in searchings for an imaginary mouse — but so would conduct his fictitious quest for that supposititious animal as eventually to achieve for himself a strategic position close behind Madame Jolicœur's chair. Then, dramatically, the pleasing end of the game would come: as the Shah de Perse — leaping with the distinguishing grace and lightness of his Persian race — would flash upward and "surprise" Madame Jolicœur by crowning her white-capped head with his small black person, all a-shake with triumphant purrs! It was a charming little comedy — and so well understood by the Shah de Perse that he never ventured to essay it under other, and more intimate, conditions of night-cap use; even as he never failed to engage in it with spirit when his white lure properly was set for him above the back of Madame Jolicœur's chair. It was as though to the Shah de Perse the white night-cap of Madame Jolicœur, displayed in accordance with the rules of the game, were an oriflamme: akin to, but in minor points differing from, the helmet of Navarre.

Being such a cat, it will be perceived that Madame Jolicœur had reason in her avowed intention to bestow upon him all of the bestowable affection remnant in her withered heart's devastated recesses; and, equally, that she would not be wholly desolate, having such a cat to comfort her, while standing impartially attendant upon the decrees of fate.

*****

To assert that any woman not conspicuously old and quite conspicuously of a fresh plumpness could be left in any city isolate, save for a cat's company, while the fates were spinning new threads for her, would be to put a severe strain upon credulity. To make that assertion specifically of Madame Jolicœur, and specifically — of all cities in the world! — of Marseille, would be to strain credulity fairly to the breaking point. On the other hand, to assert that Madame Jolicœur, in defence of her isolation, was disposed to plant machine-guns in the doorway of her dwelling — a house of modest elegance on the Pavé d'Amour, at the crossing of the Rue Bausset — would be to go too far. Nor indeed — aside from the fact that the presence of such engines of destruction would not have been tolerated by the other residents of the quietly respectable Pavé d'Amour — was Madame Jolicœur herself, as has been intimated, temperamentally inclined to go to such lengths as machine-guns in maintenance of her somewhat waveringly desired privacy in a merely cat-enlivened solitude.

Between these widely separated extremes of conjectural possibility lay the mediate truth of the matter: which truth — thus resembling precious gold in its valueless rock matrix — lay embedded in, and was to be extracted from, the irresponsible utterances of the double row of loosely hung tongues, always at hot wagging, ranged along the two sides of the Rue Bausset.

Madame Jouval, a milliner of repute — delivering herself with the generosity due to a good customer from whom an order for a trousseau was a not unremote possibility, yet with the acumen perfected by her professional experiences — summed her views of the situation, in talk with Madame Vic, proprietor of the Vic bakery, in these words: "It is of the convenances, and equally is it of her own melancholy necessities, that this poor Madame retires for a season to sorrow in a suitable seclusion in the company of her sympathetic cat. Only in such retreat can she give vent fitly to her desolating grief. But after storm comes sunshine: and I am happily assured by her less despairing appearance, and by the new mourning that I have been making for her, that even now, from the bottomless depth of her affliction, she looks beyond the storm."

"I well believe it!" snapped Madame Vic. "That the appearance of Madame Jolicœur at any time has been despairing is a matter that has escaped my notice. As to the mourning that she now wears, it is a defiance of all propriety. Why, with no more than that of colour in her frock" — Madame Vic upheld her thumb and finger infinitesimally separated — "and with a mere pin-point of a flower in her bonnet, she would be fit for the opera!"

Madame Vic spoke with a caustic bitterness that had its roots. Her own venture in second marriage had been catastrophic — so catastrophic that her neglected bakery had gone very much to the bad. Still more closely to the point, Madame Jolicœur — incident to finding entomologic specimens misplaced in her breakfast-rolls — had taken the leading part in an interchange of incivilities with the bakery's proprietor, and had withdrawn from it her custom.

"And even were her mournings not a flouting of her short year of widowhood," continued Madame Vic, with an acrimony that abbreviated the term of widowhood most unfairly — "the scores of eligible suitors who openly come streaming to her door, and are welcomed there, are as trumpets proclaiming her audacious intentions and her indecorous desires. Even Monsieur Brisson is in that outrageous procession! Is it not enough that she should entice a repulsively bald-headed notary and an old rake of a major to make their brazen advances, without suffering this anatomy of a pharmacien to come treading on their heels? — he with his hands imbrued in the life-blood of the unhappy old woman whom his mismade prescription sent in agony to the tomb! Pah! I have no patience with her! She and her grief and her seclusion and her sympathetic cat, indeed! It all is a tragedy of indiscretion — that shapes itself as a revolting farce!"

It will be observed that Madame Vic, in framing her bill of particulars, practically reduced her alleged scores of Madame Jolicœur's suitors to precisely two — since the bad third was handicapped so heavily by that notorious matter of the mismade prescription as to be a negligible quantity, quite out of the race. Indeed, it was only the preposterous temerity of Monsieur Brisson — despairingly clutching at any chance to retrieve his broken fortunes — that put him in the running at all. With the others, in such slighting terms referred to by Madame Vic — Monsieur Peloux, a notary of standing, and the Major Gontard, of the Twenty-ninth of the Line — the case was different. It had its sides.

"That this worthy lady reasonably may desire again to wed," declared Monsieur Fromagin, actual proprietor of the Épicerie Russe — an establishment liberally patronized by Madame Joli-cœur — "is as true as that when she goes to make her choosings between these estimable gentlemen she cannot make a choice that is wrong."

Madame Gauthier, a clear-starcher of position, to whom Monsieur Fromagin thus addressed himself, was less broadly positive. "That is a matter of opinion," she answered; and added: "To go no further than the very beginning, Monsieur should perceive that her choice has exactly fifty chances in the hundred of going wrong: lying, as it does, between a meagre, sallow-faced creature of a death-white baldness, and a fine big pattern of a man, strong and ruddy, with a close-clipped but abundant thatch on his head, and a moustache that admittedly is superb!"

"Ah, there speaks the woman!" said Monsieur Fromagin, with a patronizing smile distinctly irritating. "Madame will recognize — if she will but bring herself to look a little beyond the mere outside — that what I have advanced is not a matter of opinion but of fact. Observe: Here is Monsieur Peloux — to whose trifling leanness and aristocratic baldness the thoughtful give no attention — easily a notary in the very first rank. As we all know, his services are sought in cases of the most exigent importance — "

"For example," interrupted Madame Gauthier, "the case of the insurance solicitor, in whose countless defraudings my own brother was a sufferer: a creature of a vileness, whose deserts were unnumbered ages of dungeons — and who, thanks to the chicaneries of Monsieur Peloux, at this moment walks free as air!"

"It is of the professional duty of advocates," replied Monsieur Fromagin, sententiously, "to defend their clients; on the successful discharge of that duty — irrespective of minor details — depends their fame. Madame neglects the fact that Monsieur Peloux, by his masterly conduct of the case that she specifies, won for himself from his legal colleagues an immense applause."

"The more shame to his legal colleagues!" commented Madame Gauthier curtly.

"But leaving that affair quite aside," continued Monsieur Fromagin airily, but with insistence, "here is this notable advocate who reposes his important homages at Madame Jolicœur's feet: he a man of an age that is suitable, without being excessive; who has in the community an assured position; whose more than moderate wealth is known. I insist, therefore, that should she accept his homages she would do well."

"And I insist," declared Madame Gauthier stoutly, "that should she turn her back upon the Major Gontard she would do most ill!"

"Madame a little disregards my premises," Monsieur Fromagin spoke in a tone of forbearance, "and therefore a little argues — it is the privilege of her sex — against the air. Distinctly, I do not exclude from Madame Jolicœur's choice that gallant Major: whose rank — now approaching him to the command of a regiment, and fairly equalling the position at the bar achieved by Monsieur Peloux — has been won, grade by grade, by deeds of valour in his African campaignings which have made him conspicuous even in the army that stands first in such matters of all the armies of the world. Moreover — although, admittedly, in that way Monsieur Peloux makes a better showing — he is of an easy affluence. On the Camargue he has his excellent estate in vines, from which comes a revenue more than sufficing to satisfy more than modest wants. At Les Martigues he has his charming coquette villa, smothered in the flowers of his own planting, to which at present he makes his agreeable escapes from his military duties; and in which, when his retreat is taken, he will pass softly his sunset years. With these substantial points in his favour, the standing of the Major Gontard in this matter practically is of a parity with the standing of Monsieur Peloux. Equally, both are worthy of Madame Jolicœur's consideration: both being able to continue her in the life of elegant comfort to which she is accustomed; and both being on a social plane — it is of her level accurately — to which the widow of an ingénieur des ponts et chaus-sées neither steps up nor steps down. Having now made clear, I trust, my reasonings, I repeat the proposition with which Madame took issue: When Madame Jolicœur goes to make her choosings between these estimable gentlemen she cannot make a choice that is wrong."

"And I repeat, Monsieur," said Madame Gauthier, lifting her basket from the counter, "that in making her choosings Madame Jolicœur either goes to raise herself to the heights of a matured happiness, or to plunge herself into bald-headed abysses of de-spair. Yes, Monsieur, that far apart are her choosings!" And Madame Gauthier added, in communion with herself as she passed to the street with her basket: "As for me, it would be that adorable Major by a thousand times!"

*****

As was of reason, since hers was the first place in the matter, Madame Jolicœur herself carried on debatings — in the portion of her heart that had escaped complete devastation — identical in essence with the debatings of her case which went up and down the Rue Bausset.

Not having become dévote — in the year and more of oppor-tunity open to her for a turn in that direction — one horn of her original dilemma had been eliminated, so to say, by atrophy. Being neglected, it had withered: with the practical result that out of her very indecisions had come a decisive choice. But to her new dilemma, of which the horns were the Major and the Notary — in the privacy of her secret thoughts she made no bones of admitting that this dilemma confronted her — the atrophying process was not applicable; at least, not until it could be applied with a sharp finality. Too long dallied with, it very well might lead to the atrophy of both of them in dudgeon; and thence on-ward, conceivably, to her being left to cling only to the Shah de Perse for all the remainder of her days.

Therefore, to the avoidance of that too radical conclusion, Madame Jolicœur engaged in her debatings briskly: offering to herself, in effect, the balanced arguments advanced by Monsieur Fromagin in favour equally of Monsieur Peloux and of the Major Gontard; taking as her own, with moderating exceptions and emendations, the views of Madame Gauthier as to the meagreness and pallid baldness of the one and the sturdiness and gallant bearing of the other; considering, from the standpoint of her own personal knowledge in the premises, the Notary's disposition toward a secretive reticence that bordered upon severity, in contrast with the cordially frank and debonair temperament of the Major; and, at the back of all, keeping well in mind the fundamental truths that opportunity ever is evanescent and that time ever is on the wing.

As the result of her debatings, and not less as the result of experience gained in her earlier campaigning, Madame Jolicœur took up a strategic position nicely calculated to inflame the desire for, by assuming the uselessness of, an assault. In set terms, confirming particularly her earlier and more general avowal, she declared equally to the Major and to the Notary that absolutely the whole of her bestowable affection — of the remnant in her withered heart available for distribution — was bestowed upon the Shah de Perse: and so, with an alluring nonchalance, left them to draw the logical conclusion that their strivings to win that desirable quantity were idle — since a definite disposition of it already had been made.

The reply of the Major Gontard to this declaration was in keeping with his known amiability, but also was in keeping with his military habit of command. "Assuredly," he said, "Madame shall continue to bestow, within reason, her affections upon Monsieur le Shah; and with them that brave animal — he is a cat of ten thousand — shall have my affections as well. Already, knowing my feeling for him, we are friends — as Madame shall see to her own convincing." Addressing himself in tones of kindly persuasion to the Shah de Perse, he added: "Viens, Monsieur!" — whereupon the Shah de Perse instantly jumped himself to the Major's knee and broke forth, in response to a savant rubbing of his soft little jowls, into his gurgling purr. "Voilà, Madame!" continued the Major. "It is to be perceived that we have our good understandings, the Shah de Perse and I. That we all shall live happily together tells itself without words. But observe" — of a sudden the voice of the Major thrilled with a deep earnestness, and his style of address changed to a familiarity that only the intensity of his feeling condoned — "I am resolved that to me, above all, shall be given thy dear affections. Thou shalt give me the perfect flower of them — of that fact rest thou assured. In thy heart I am to be the very first — even as in my heart thou thyself art the very first of all the world. In Africa I have had my successes in my conquests and holdings of fortresses. Believe me, I shall have an equal success in conquering and in holding the sweetest fortress in France!"

Certainly, the Major Gontard had a bold way with him. But that it had its attractions, not to say its compellings, Madame Jolicœur could not honestly deny.

On the part of the Notary — whose disposition, fostered by his profession, was toward subtlety rather than toward boldness — Madame Jolicœur's declaration of cat rights was received with no such belligerent blare of trumpets and beat of drums. He met it with a light show of banter — beneath which, to come to the surface later, lay hidden dark thoughts.

"Madame makes an excellent pleasantry," he said with a smile of the blandest. "Without doubt, not a very flattering pleasantry — but I know that her denial of me in favour of her cat is but a jesting at which we both may laugh. And we may laugh together the better because, in the roots of her jesting, we have our sympathies. I also have an intensity of affection for cats" — to be just to Monsieur Peloux, who loathed cats, it must be said that he gulped as he made this flagrantly untruthful statement — "and with this admirable cat, so dear to Madame, it goes to make itself that we speedily become enduring friends."

Curiously enough — a mere coincidence, of course — as the Notary uttered these words so sharply at points with veracity, in the very moment of them, the Shah de Perse stiffly retired into his sulkiest corner and turned what had every appearance of being a scornful back upon the world.

Judiciously ignoring this inopportunely equivocal incident, Monsieur Peloux reverted to the matter in chief and concluded his deliverance in these words: "I well understand, I repeat, that Madame for the moment makes a comedy of herself and of her cat for my amusing. But I persuade myself that her droll fancyings will not be lasting, and that she will be serious with me in the end. Until then — and then most of all — I am at her feet humbly: an unworthy, but a very earnest, suppliant for her goodwill. Should she have the cruelty to refuse my supplication, it will remain with me to die in an unmerited despair!"

Certainly, this was an appeal — of a sort. But even without perceiving the mitigating subtlety of its comminative final clause — so skilfully worded as to leave Monsieur Peloux free to bring off his threatened unmeritedly despairing death quite at his own convenience — Madame Jolicœur did not find it satisfying. In contrast with the Major Gontard's ringingly audacious declarations of his habits in dealing with fortresses, she felt that it lacked force. And, also — this, of course, was a sheer weakness — she permitted herself to be influenced appreciably by the indicated preferences of the Shah de Perse: who had jumped to the knee of the Major with an affectionate alacrity; and who undeniably had turned on the Notary — either by chance or by intention — a back of scorn.

As the general outcome of these several developments, Madame Jolicœur's debatings came to have in them — if I so may state the trend of her mental activities — fewer bald heads and more moustaches; and her never severely set purpose to abide in a loneliness relieved only by the Shah de Perse was abandoned root and branch.

*****

While Madame Jolicœur continued her debatings — which, in their modified form, manifestly were approaching her to conclusions — water was running under bridges elsewhere.

In effect, her hesitancies produced a period of suspense that gave opportunity for, and by the exasperating delay of it stimulated, the resolution of the Notary's dark thoughts into darker deeds. With reason, he did not accept at its face value Madame Jolicœur's declaration touching the permanent bestowal of her remnant affections; but he did believe that there was enough in it to make the Shah de Perse a delaying obstacle to his own acquisition of them. When obstacles got in this gentleman's way it was his habit to kick them out of it — a habit that had not been unduly stunted by half a lifetime of successful practice at the criminal bar.

Because of his professional relations with them, Monsieur Peloux had an extensive acquaintance among criminals of varying shades of intensity — at times, in his dubious doings, they could be useful to him — hidden away in the shadowy nooks and corners of the city; and he also had his emissaries through whom they could be reached. All the conditions thus standing attendant upon his convenience, it was a facile matter for him to make an appointment with one of these disreputables at a cabaret of bad record in the Quartier de la Tourette: a region — bordering upon the north side of the Vieux Port — that is at once the oldest and the foulest quarter of Marseille.

In going to keep this appointment — as was his habit on such occasions, in avoidance of possible spying upon his movements — he went deviously: taking a cab to the Bassin de Carènage, as though some maritime matter engaged him, and thence making the transit of the Vieux Port in a bateau mouche. It was while crossing in the ferryboat that a sudden shuddering beset him: as he perceived with horror — but without repentance — the pit into which he descended. In his previous, always professional, meetings with criminals his position had been that of unassailable dominance. In his pending meeting — since he himself would be not only a criminal but an inciter to crime — he would be, in the essence of the matter, the under dog. Beneath his seemly black hat his bald head went whiter than even its normal deathly whiteness, and perspiration started from its every pore. Almost with a groan, he removed his hat and dried with his handkerchief what were in a way his tears of shame.

Over the interview between Monsieur Peloux and his hireling — cheerfully moistened, on the side of the hireling, with absinthe of a vileness in keeping with its place of purchase — decency demands the partial drawing of a veil. In brief, Monsieur Peloux — his guilty eyes averted, the shame-tears streaming afresh from his bald head — presented his criminal demand and stated the sum that he would pay for its gratification. This sum — being in keeping with his own estimate of what it paid for — was so much in excess of the hireling's views concerning the value of a mere cat-killing that he fairly jumped at it.

"Be not disturbed, Monsieur!" he replied, with the fervour of one really grateful, and with the expansive extravagance of a Marseillais keyed up with exceptionally bad absinthe. "Be not disturbed in the smallest! In this very coming moment this camel of a cat shall die a thousand deaths; and in but another moment immeasurable quantities of salt and ashes shall obliterate his justly despicable grave! To an instant accomplishment of Monsieur's wishes I pledge whole-heartedly the word of an honest man."

Actually — barring the number of deaths to be inflicted on the Shah de Perse, and the needlessly defiling concealment of his burial-place — this radical treatment of the matter was precisely what Monsieur Peloux desired; and what, in terms of innuendo and euphuism, he had asked for. But the brutal frankness of the hireling, and his evident delight in sinning for good wages, came as an arousing shock to the enfeebled remnant of the Notary's better nature — with a resulting vacillation of purpose to which he would have risen superior had he been longer habituated to the ways of crime.

"No! No!" he said weakly. "I did not mean that — by no means all of that. At least — that is to say — you will understand me, my good man, that enough will be done if you remove the cat from Marseille. Yes, that is what I mean — take it somewhere. Take it to Cassis, to Arles, to Avignon — where you will — and leave it there. The railway ticket is my charge — and, also, you have an extra napoléon for your refreshment by the way. Yes, that suffices. In a bag, you know — and soon!"

Returning across the Vieux Port in the bateau mouche, Monsieur Peloux no longer shuddered in dread of crime to be committed — his shuddering was for accomplished crime. On his bald head, unheeded, the gushing tears of shame accumulated in pools.

*****

When leaves of absence permitted him to make retirements to his coquette little estate at Les Martigues, the Major Gontard was as another Cincinnatus: with the minor differences that the lickerish cookings of the brave Marthe — his old femme de ménage: a veritable protagonist among cooks, even in Provence — checked him on the side of severe simplicity; that he would have welcomed with effusion lictors, or others, come to announce his advance to a regiment; and that he made no use whatever of a plow.

In the matter of the plow, he had his excuses. His two or three acres of land lay on a hillside banked in tiny terraces — quite unsuited to the use of that implement — and the whole of his agricultural energies were given to the cultivation of flowers. Among his flowers, intelligently assisted by old Michel, he worked with a zeal bred of his affection for them; and after his workings, when the cool of evening was come, smoked his pipe refreshingly while seated on the vine-bowered estrade before his trim villa on the crest of the slope: the while sniffing with a just interest at the fumes of old Marthe's cookings, and placidly delighting in the ever-new beauties of the sunsets above the distant mountains and their near-by reflected beauties in the waters of the Étang de Berre.

Save in his professional relations with recalcitrant inhabitants of Northern Africa, he was of a gentle nature, this amiable warrior: ever kindly, when kindliness was deserved, in all his dealings with mankind. Equally, his benevolence was extended to the lower orders of animals — that it was understood, and reciprocated, the willing jumping of the Shah de Perse to his friendly knee made manifest — and was exhibited in practical ways. Naturally, he was a liberal contributor to the funds of the Société protectrice des animaux; and, what was more to the purpose, it was his well-rooted habit to do such protecting as was necessary, on his own account, when he chanced upon any suffering creature in trouble or in pain.

Possessing these commendable characteristics, it follows that the doings of the Major Gontard in the railway station at Pas de Lanciers — on the day sequent to the day on which Monsieur Peloux was the promoter of a criminal conspiracy — could not have been other than they were. Equally does it follow that his doings produced the doings of the man with the bag.

Pas de Lanciers is the little station at which one changes trains in going from Marseille to Les Martigues. Descending from a first-class carriage, the Major Gontard awaited the Martigues train — his leave was for two days, and his thoughts were engaged pleasantly with the breakfast that old Marthe would have ready for him and with plans for his flowers. From a third-class carriage descended the man with the bag, who also awaited the Martigues train. Presently — the two happening to come together in their saunterings up and down the platform — the Major's interest was aroused by observing that within the bag went on a persistent wriggling; and his interest was quickened into characteristic action when he heard from its interior, faintly but quite distinctly, a very pitiful half-strangled little mew!

"In another moment," said the Major, addressing the man sharply, "that cat will be suffocated. Open the bag instantly and give it air!"

"Pardon, Monsieur," replied the man, starting guiltily. "This excellent cat is not suffocating. In the bag it breathes freely with all its lungs. It is a pet cat, having the habitude to travel in this manner; and, because it is of a friendly disposition, it is accustomed thus to make its cheerful little remarks." By way of comment upon this explanation, there came from the bag another half-strangled mew that was not at all suggestive of cheerfulness. It was a faint miserable mew — that told of cat despair!

At that juncture a down train came in on the other side of the platform, a train on its way to Marseille.

"Thou art a brute!" said the Major, tersely. "I shall not suffer thy cruelties to continue!" As he spoke, he snatched away the bag from its uneasy possessor and applied himself to untying its confining cord. Oppressed by the fear that goes with evil-doing, the man hesitated for a moment before attempting to retrieve what constructively was his property.

In that fateful moment the bag opened and a woebegone little black cat-head appeared; and then the whole of a delighted little black cat-body emerged — and cuddled with joy-purrs of recognition in its deliverer's arms! Within the sequent instant the recognition was mutual. "Thunder of guns!" cried the Major. "It is the Shah de Perse!"

Being thus caught red-handed, the hireling of Monsieur Peloux cowered. "Brigand!" continued the Major. "Thou hast ravished away this charming cat by the foulest of robberies. Thou art worse than the scum of Arab camp-followings. And if I had thee to myself, over there in the desert," he added grimly, "thou shouldst go the same way!"

All overawed by the Major's African attitude, the hireling took to whining. "Monsieur will believe me when I tell him that I am but an unhappy tool — I, an honest man whom a rich tempter, taking advantage of my unmerited poverty, has betrayed into crime. Monsieur himself shall judge me when I have told him all!" And then — with creditably imaginative variations on the theme of a hypothetical dying wife in combination with six supposititious starving children — the man came close enough to telling all to make clear that his backer in cat-stealing was Monsieur Peloux!

With a gasp of astonishment, the Major again took the word. "What matters it, animal, by whom thy crime was prompted? Thou art the perpetrator of it — and to thee comes punishment! Shackles and prisons are in store for thee! I shall — "

But what the Major Gontard had in mind to do toward assisting the march of retributive justice is immaterial — since he did not do it. Even as he spoke — in these terms of doom that qualifying conditions rendered doomless — the man suddenly dodged past him, bolted across the platform, jumped to the foot-board of a carriage of the just-starting train, cleverly bundled himself through an open window, and so was gone: leaving the Major standing lonely, with impotent rage filling his heart, and with the Shah de Perse all a purring cuddle in his arms!

Acting on a just impulse, the Major Gontard sped to the tele-graph office. Two hours must pass before he could follow the miscreant; but the departed train ran express to Marseille, and telegraphic heading-off was possible. To his flowers, and to the romance of a breakfast that old Marthe by then was in the very act of preparing for him, his thoughts went in bitter relinquish-ment: but his purpose was stern! Plumping the Shah de Perse down anyway on the telegraph table, and seizing a pen fiercely, he began his writings. And then, of a sudden, an inspiration came to him that made him stop in his writings — and that changed his flames of anger into flames of joy.

His first act under the influence of this new and better emo-tion was to tear his half-finished dispatch into fragments. His second act was to assuage the needs, physical and psychical, of the Shah de Perse — near to collapse for lack of food and drink, and his little cat feelings hurt by his brusque deposition on the telegraph table — by carrying him tenderly to the buffet; and there — to the impolitely over-obvious amusement of the buf-fetière — purchasing cream without stint for the allaying of his famishings. To his feasting the Shah de Perse went with the avid energy begotten of his bag-compelled long fast. Dipping his little red tongue deep into the saucer, he lapped with a vigour that all cream-splattered his little black nose. Yet his admirable little cat manners were not forgotten: even in the very thick of his eager lappings — pathetically eager, in view of the cause of them — he purred forth gratefully, with a gurgling chokiness, his earnest little cat thanks.

As the Major Gontard watched this pleasing spectacle his heart was all aglow within him and his face was of a radiance comparable only with that of an Easter-morning sun. To himself he was saying: "It is a dream that has come to me! With the dis-graced enemy in retreat, and with the Shah de Perse for my banner, it is that I hold victoriously the whole universe in the hollow of my hand!"

*****

While stopping appreciably short of claiming for himself a clutch upon the universe, Monsieur Peloux also had his satisfactions on the evening of the day that had witnessed the enlèvement of the Shah de Perse. By his own eyes he knew certainly that that iniquitous kidnapping of a virtuous cat had been effected. In the morning the hireling had brought to him in his private office the unfortunate Shah de Perse — all unhappily bagged, and even then giving vent to his pathetic complainings — and had exhibited him, as a pièce justificatif, when making his demand for railway fare and the promised extra napolèon. In the mid-afternoon the hireling had returned, with the satisfying announcement that all was accomplished: that he had carried the cat to Pas de Lanciers, of an adequate remoteness, and there had left him with a person in need of a cat who received him willingly. Being literally true, this statement had in it so convincing a ring of sincerity that Monsieur Peloux paid down in full the blood-money and dismissed his bravo with commendation. Thereafter, being alone, he rubbed his hands — gladly thinking of what was in the way to happen in sequence to the permanent removal of this cat stumbling-block from his path. Although professionally accustomed to consider the possibilities of permutation, the known fact that petards at times are retroactive did not present itself to his mind.

And yet — being only an essayist in crime, still unhardened — certain compunctions beset him as he approached himself, on the to-be eventful evening of that eventful day, to the door of Madame Jolicœur's modestly elegant dwelling on the Pavé d'Amour. In the back of his head were justly self-condemnatory thoughts, to the general effect that he was a blackguard and deserved to be kicked. In the dominant front of his head, however, were thoughts of a more agreeable sort: of how he would find Madame Jolicœur all torn and rent by the bitter sorrow of her bereavement; of how he would pour into her harried heart a flood of sympathy by which that injured organ would be soothed and mollified; of how she would be lured along gently to requite his tender condolence with a softening gratitude — that presently would merge easily into the yet softer phrase of love! It was a well-made program, and it had its kernel of reason in his recognized ability to win bad causes — as that of the insurance solicitor — by emotional pleadings which in the same breath lured to lenience and made the intrinsic demerits of the cause obscure.

"Madame dines," was the announcement that met Monsieur Peloux when, in response to his ring, Madame Jolicœur's door was opened for him by a trim maid-servant. "But Madame already has continued so long her dining," added the maid-servant, with a glint in her eyes that escaped his preoccupied attention, "that in but another instant must come the end. If M'sieu' will have the amiability to await her in the salon, it will be for but a point of time!"

Between this maid-servant and Monsieur Peloux no love was lost. Instinctively he was aware of, and resented, her views — practically identical with those expressed by Madame Gauthier to Monsieur Fromagin — touching his deserts as compared with the deserts of the Major Gontard. Moreover, she had personal incentives to take her revenges. From Monsieur Peloux, her only vail had been a miserable two-franc Christmas box. From the Major, as from a perpetually verdant Christmas-tree, boxes of bonbons and five-franc pieces at all times descended upon her in showers.

Without perceiving the curious smile that accompanied this young person's curiously cordial invitation to enter, he accepted the invitation and was shown into the salon: where he seated himself — a left-handedness of which he would have been incapable had he been less perturbed — in Madame Jolicœur's own special chair. An anatomical vagary of the Notary's meagre person was the undue shortness of his body and the undue length of his legs. Because of this eccentricity of proportion, his bald head rose above the back of the chair to a height approximately identical with that of its normal occupant.

His waiting time — extending from its promised point to

what seemed to him to be a whole geographical meridian — went slowly. To relieve it, he took a book from the table, and in a desultory manner turned the leaves. While thus perfunctorily engaged, he heard the clicking of an opening door, and then the sound of voices: of Madame Jolicœur's voice, and of a man's voice — which latter, coming nearer, he recognized beyond all doubting as the voice of the Major Gontard. Of other voices there was not a sound: whence the compromising fact was obvious that the two had gone through that long dinner together, and alone! Knowing, as he did, Madame Jolicœur's habitual disposition toward the convenances — willingly to be boiled in oil rather than in the smallest particular to abrade them — he perceived that only two explanations of the situation were possible: either she had lapsed of a sudden into madness; or — the thought was petrifying — the Major Gontard had won out in his French campaigning on his known conquering African lines. The cheerfully sane tone of the lady's voice forbade him to clutch at the poor solace to be found in the first alternative — and so forced him to accept the second. Yielding for a moment to his emotions, the death-whiteness of his bald head taking on a still deathlier pallor, Monsieur Peloux buried his face in his hands and groaned.

In that moment of his obscured perception a little black personage trotted into the salon on soundless paws. Quite possibly, in his then overwrought condition, had Monsieur Peloux seen this personage enter he would have shrieked — in the confident belief that before him was a cat ghost! Pointedly, it was not a ghost. It was the happy little Shah de Perse himself — all a-frisk with the joy of his blessed home-coming and very much alive! Knowing, as I do, many of the mysterious ways of little cat souls, I even venture to believe that his overbubbling gladness largely was due to his sympathetic perception of the gladness that his home-coming had brought to two human hearts.

Certainly, all through that long dinner the owners of those hearts had done their best, by their pettings and their pamperings of him, to make him a participant in their deep happiness; and he, gratefully respondent, had made his affectionate thankings by going through all of his repertory of tricks — with one exception

— again and again. Naturally, his great trick, while unexhibited, repeatedly had been referred to. Blushing delightfully, Madame Jolicœur had told about the night-cap that was a necessary part of it; and had promised — blushing still more delightfully — that at some time, in the very remote future, the Major should see it performed. For my own part, because of my knowledge of little cat souls, I am persuaded that the Shah de Perse, while missing the details of this love-laughing talk, did get into his head the general trend of it; and therefore did trot on in advance into the salon with his little cat mind full of the notion that Madame Jolicœur immediately would follow him — to seat herself, duly night-capped, book in hand, in signal for their game of surprises to begin.

Unconscious of the presence of the Shah de Perse, tortured by the gay tones of the approaching voices, clutching his book vengefully as though it were a throat, his bald head beaded with the sweat of agony and the pallor of it intensified by his poignant emotion, Monsieur Peloux sat rigid in Madame Jolicœur's chair!

*****

"It is declared," said Monsieur Brisson, addressing himself to Madame Jouval, for whom he was in the act of preparing what was spoken of between them as "the tonic," a courteous euphuism, "that that villain Notary, aided by a bandit hired to his assistance, was engaged in administering poison to the cat; and that the brave animal, freeing itself from the bandit's holdings, tore to destruction the whole of his bald head — and then triumphantly escaped to its home!"

"A sight to see is that head of his!" replied Madame Jouval. "So swathed is it in bandages, that the turban of the Grand Turk is less!" Madame Jouval spoke in tones of satisfaction that were of reason — already she had held conferences with Madame Jolicœur in regard to the trousseau.

"And all," continued Monsieur Brisson, with rancour, "because of his jealousies of the cat's place in Madame Jolicœur's affections — the affections which he so hopelessly hoped, forgetful of his own repulsiveness, to win for himself!"

"Ah, she has done well, that dear lady," said Madame Jouval warmly. "As between the Notary — repulsive, as Monsieur justly terms him — and the charming Major, her instincts rightly have directed her. To her worthy cat, who aided in her choosing, she has reason to be grateful. Now her cruelly wounded heart will find solace. That she should wed again, and happily, was Heaven's will."

"It was the will of the baggage herself!" declared Monsieur Brisson with bitterness. "Hardly had she put on her travesty of a mourning than she began her oglings of whole armies of men!"

Aside from having confected with her own hands the mourning to which Monsieur Brisson referred so disparagingly, Madame Jouval was not one to hear calmly the ascription of the term baggage — the word has not lost in its native French, as it has lost in its naturalized English, its original epithetical intensity — to a patroness from whom she was in the very article of receiving an order for an exceptionally rich trousseau. Naturally, she bristled. "Monsieur must admit at least," she said sharply, "that her oglings did not come in his direction;" and with an irritatingly smooth sweetness added: "As to the dealings of Monsieur Peloux with the cat, Monsieur doubtless speaks with an assured knowledge. Remembering, as we all do, the affair of the unhappy old woman, it is easy to perceive that to Monsieur, above all others, any one in need of poisonings would come!"

The thrust was so keen that for the moment Monsieur Brisson met it only with a savage glare. Then the bottle that he handed to Madame Jouval inspired him with an answer. "Madame is in error," he said with politeness. "For poisons it is possible to go variously elsewhere — as, for example, to Madame's tongue." Had he stopped with that retort courteous, but also searching, he would have done well. He did ill by adding to it the retort brutal: "But that old women of necessity come to me for their hair-dyes is another matter. That much I grant to Madame with all good will."

Admirably restraining herself, Madame Jouval replied in

tones of sympathy: "Monsieur receives my commiserations in his misfortunes." Losing a large part of her restraint, she continued, her eyes glittering: "Yet Monsieur's temperament clearly is over-sanguine. It is not less than a miracle of absurdity that he imagined: that he, weighted down with his infamous murderings of scores of innocent old women, had even a chance the most meagre of realizing his ridiculous aspirations of Madame Jolicœur's hand!" Snatching up her bottle and making for the door, without any restraint whatever she added: "Monsieur and his aspirations are a tragedy of stupidity — and equally are abounding in all the materials for a farce at the Palais de Cristal!"

Monsieur Brisson was cut off from opportunity to reply to this outburst by Madame Jouval's abrupt departure. His loss of opportunity had its advantages. An adequate reply to her discharge of such a volley of home truths would have been difficult to frame.

*****

In the Vic bakery, between Madame Vic and Monsieur Fromagin, a discussion was in hand akin to that carried on between Monsieur Brisson and Madame Jouval — but marked with a somewhat nearer approach to accuracy in detail. Being sequent to the settlement of Monsieur Fromagin's monthly bill — always a matter of nettling dispute — it naturally tended to develop its own asperities.

"They say," observed Monsieur Fromagin, "that the cat — it was among his many tricks — had the habitude to jump on Madame Jolicœur's head when, for that purpose, she covered it with a night-cap. The use of the cat's claws on such a covering, and, also, her hair being very abundant — "

"*Very* abundant!" interjected Madame Vic; and added: "She, she is of a richness to buy wigs by the scores!"

"It was his custom, I say," continued Monsieur Fromagin with insistence, "to steady himself after his leap by using lightly his claws. His illusion in regard to the bald head of the Notary, it would seem, led to the catastrophe. Using his claws at first lightly, according to his habit, he went on to use them with a truly savage energy — when he found himself as on ice on that slippery eminence and verging to a fall."

"They say that his scalp was peeled away in strips and strings!" said Madame Vic. "And all the while that woman and that reprobate of a Major standing by in shrieks and roars of laughter — never raising a hand to save him from the beast's ferocities! The poor man has my sympathies. He, at least, in all his doings — I do not for a moment believe the story that he caused the cat to be stolen — observed rigidly the convenances: so recklessly shattered by Madame Jolicœur in her most compromising dinner with the Major alone!"

"But Madame forgets that their dinner was in celebration of their betrothal — following Madame Jolicœur's glad yielding, in just gratitude, when the Major heroically had rescued her deserving cat from the midst of its enemies and triumphantly had restored it to her arms."

"It is the man's part," responded Madame Vic, "to make the best of such matters. In the eyes of all right-minded women her conduct has been of a shamelessness from first to last: tossing and balancing the two of them for months upon months; luring them, and countless others with them, to her feet; declaring always that for her disgusting cat's sake she will have none of them; and ending by pretending brazenly that for her cat's sake she bestows herself — second-hand remnant that she is — on the handsomest man for his age, concerning his character it is well to be silent; that she could find for herself in all Marseille! On such actions, on such a woman, Monsieur, the saints in heaven look down with an agonized scorn!"

"Only those of the saints, Madame," said Monsieur Fromagin, warmly taking up the cudgels for his best customer, "as in the matter of second marriages, prior to their arrival in heaven, have had regrettable experiences. Equally, I venture to assert, a like qualification applies to a like attitude on earth. That Madame has her prejudices, incident to her misfortunes, is known."

"That Monsieur has his brutalities, incident to his regrettable bad breeding, also is known. His present offensiveness, however, passes all limits. I request him to remove himself from my sight." Madame Vic spoke with dignity.

Speaking with less dignity, but with conviction — as Monsieur Fromagin left the bakery — she added: "Monsieur, effectively, is a camel! I bestow upon him my disdain!"

Thomas A. Janvier.

A FRIENDLY RAT

Most of our animals, also many creeping things, such as our "wilde wormes in woods," common toads, natter-jacks, newts, and lizards, and stranger still, many insects, have been tamed and kept as pets.

Badgers, otters, foxes, hares, and voles are easily dealt with; but that any person should desire to fondle so prickly a creature as a hedgehog, or so diabolical a mammalian as the bloodthirsty flat-headed little weasel, seems very odd. Spiders, too, are uncomfortable pets; you can't caress them as you could a dormouse; the most you can do is to provide your spider with a clear glass bottle to live in, and teach him to come out in response to a musical sound, drawn from a banjo or fiddle, to take a fly from your fingers and go back again to its bottle.

An acquaintance of the writer is partial to adders as pets, and he handles them as freely as the schoolboy does his innocuous ring-snake; Mr. Benjamin Kidd once gave us a delightful account of his pet humble-bees, who used to fly about his room, and come at call to be fed, and who manifested an almost painful interest in his coat buttons, examining them every day as if anxious to find out their true significance. Then there was my old friend, Miss Hopely, the writer on reptiles, who died recently, aged 99 years, who tamed newts, but whose favourite pet was a slow-worm. She was never tired of expatiating on its lovable qualities. One finds Viscount Grey's pet squirrels more engaging, for these are wild squirrels in a wood in Northumberland, who quickly find out when he is at home and make their way to the house, scale the walls, and invade the library; then, jumping upon his writing-table, are rewarded with nuts, which they take from his hand. Another Northumbrian friend of the writer keeps, or kept, a pet cormorant, and finds him no less greedy in the domestic than in the wild state. After catching and swallowing fish all the morning in a neighbouring river, he wings his way home at meal-times, screaming to be fed, and ready to devour all the meat and pudding he can get.

The list of strange creatures might be extended indefinitely, even fishes included; but who has ever heard of a tame pet rat? Not the small white, pink-eyed variety, artificially bred, which one may buy at any dealer's, but a common brown rat, *Mus decumanus*, one of the commonest wild animals in England and certainly the most disliked. Yet this wonder has been witnessed recently in the village of Lelant, in West Cornwall. Here is the strange story, which is rather sad and at the same time a little funny.

This was not a case of "wild nature won by kindness"; the rat simply thrust itself and its friendship on the woman of the cottage: and she, being childless and much alone in her kitchen and living-room, was not displeased at its visits: on the contrary, she fed it; in return the rat grew more and more friendly and familiar towards her, and the more familiar it grew, the more she liked the rat. The trouble was, she possessed a cat, a nice gentle animal not often at home, but it was dreadful to think of what might happen at any moment should pussy walk in when her visitor was with her. Then, one day, pussy did walk in when the rat was present, purring loudly, her tail held stiffly up, showing that she was in her usual sweet temper. On catching sight of the rat, she appeared to know intuitively that it was there as a privileged guest, while the rat on its part seemed to know, also by intuition, that it had nothing to fear. At all events these two quickly became friends and were evidently pleased to be together, as they now spent most of the time in the room, and would drink milk from the same saucer, and sleep bunched up together, and were extremely intimate.

By and by the rat began to busy herself making a nest in a corner of the kitchen under a cupboard, and it became evident that there would soon be an increase in the rat population. She now spent her time running about and gathering little straws, feathers, string, and anything of the kind she could pick up, also stealing or begging for strips of cotton, or bits of wool and thread from the work-basket. Now it happened that her friend was one of those cats with huge tufts of soft hair on the two sides of her face; a cat of that type, which is not uncommon, has a quaint resemblance to a Mid-Victorian gentleman with a pair of magnificent side-whiskers of a silky softness covering both cheeks and flowing down like a double beard. The rat suddenly discovered that this hair was just what she wanted to add a cushion-like lining to her nest, so that her naked pink little ratlings should be born into the softest of all possible worlds. At once she started plucking out the hairs, and the cat, taking it for a new kind of game, but a little too rough to please her, tried for a while to keep her head out of reach and to throw the rat off. But she wouldn't be thrown off, and as she persisted in flying back and jumping at the cat's face and plucking the hairs, the cat quite lost her temper and administered a blow with her claws unsheathed.

The rat fled to her refuge to lick her wounds, and was no doubt as much astonished at the sudden change in her friend's disposition as the cat had been at the rat's new way of showing her playfulness. The result was that when, after attending her scratches, she started upon her task of gathering soft materials, she left the cat severely alone. They were no longer friends; they simply ignored one another's presence in the room. The little ones, numbering about a dozen, presently came to light and were quietly removed by the woman's husband, who didn't mind his missis keeping a rat, but drew the line at one.

The rat quickly recovered from her loss and was the same nice affectionate little thing she had always been to her mistress; then a fresh wonder came to light — cat and rat were fast friends once more! This happy state of things lasted a few weeks; but, as we know, the rat was married, though her lord and master never appeared on the scene, indeed, he was not wanted; and very soon it became plain to see that more little rats were coming. The rat is an exceedingly prolific creature; she can give a month's start to a rabbit and beat her at the end by about 40 points.

Then came the building of the nest in the same old corner, and when it got to the last stage and the rat was busily running about in search of soft materials for the lining, she once more made the discovery that those beautiful tufts of hair on her friend's face were just what she wanted, and once more she set vigorously to work pulling the hairs out. Again, as on the former occasion, the cat tried to keep her friend off, hitting her right and left with her soft pads, and spitting a little, just to show that she didn't like it. But the rat was determined to have the hairs, and the more she was thrown off the more bent was she on getting them, until the breaking-point was reached and puss, in a sudden rage, let fly, dealing blow after blow with lightning rapidity and with all the claws out. The rat, shrieking with pain and terror, rushed out of the room and was never seen again, to the lasting grief of her mistress. But its memory will long remain like a fragrance in the cottage — perhaps the only cottage in all this land where kindly feelings for the rat are cherished.

W. H. Hudson.

MONTY'S FRIEND

The discovery of gold at Thompson's Flat, near the northern boundary of Montana, had been promptly followed by the expected rush of bold and needy adventurers. But disappointment awaited them. Undoubtedly there was gold a few feet below the surface, but it was not found in quantities sufficient to compensate for the labour, privation, and danger, which the miners were compelled to undergo.

It is true that the first discoverer of gold, who had given his name to the Flat, had found a "pocket," which had made him a rich man; but his luck remained unique, and as Big Simpson sarcastically remarked, "A man might as well try to find a pocket in a woman's dress as to search for a second pocket in Thompson's Flat." For eight months of the year the ground was frozen deep and hard, and during the brief summer the heat was intense. There were hostile Indians in the vicinity of the camp, and although little danger was to be apprehended from them while the camp swarmed with armed miners, there was every probability that they would sooner or later attack the handful of men who had remained, after the great majority of the miners had abandoned their claims and gone in search of more promising fields.

In the early part of the summer following Thompson's discovery of gold there were but thirty men left in the camp, with only a single combined grocery and saloon to minister to their wants. Partly because of obstinacy, and partly because of a want of energy to repeat the experiment of searching for gold in some other unprofitable place, these thirty men remained, and daily prosecuted their nearly hopeless search for fortune. Their evenings were spent in the saloon, but there was a conspicuous absence of anything like jollity. The men were too poor to gamble with any zest, and the whiskey of the saloon keeper was bad and dear.

The one gleam of good fortune which had come to the camp was the fact that the Indians had disappeared, having, as it was believed, gone hundreds of miles south to attack another tribe. Gradually the miners relaxed the precautions which had at first been maintained against an attack, and although every man went armed to his work, sentinels were no longer posted either by day or night, and the Gatling gun that had been bought by public subscription in the prosperous days of the camp remained in the storeroom of the saloon without ammunition, and with its mechanism rusty and immovable.

Only one miner had arrived at Thompson's Flat that summer. He was a middle-aged man who said that his name was Montgomery Carleton — a name which instantly awoke the resentment of the camp, and was speedily converted into "Monte Carlo" by the resentful miners, who intimated very plainly that no man could carry a fifteen-inch name in that camp and live. Monte Carlo, or Monty, as he was usually called, had the further distinction of being the ugliest man in the entire north-west. He had, at some unspecified time, been kicked in the face by a mule, with the result that his features were converted into a hideous mask. He seemed to be of a social disposition, and would have joined freely in the conversation which went on at the saloon, but his advances were coldly received.

Instead of pitying the man's misfortune, and avoiding all allusion to it, the miners bluntly informed him that he was too ugly to associate with gentlemen, and that a modest and retiring attitude was what public sentiment required of him. Monty took the rebuff quietly, and thereafter rarely spoke unless he was spoken to. He continued to frequent the saloon, sitting in the darkest corner, where he smoked his pipe, drank his solitary whisky, and answered with pathetic pleasure any remark that might be flung at him, even when it partook of the nature of a coarse jest at his expense.

One gloomy evening Monty entered the saloon half an hour later than usual. It had been raining all day, and the spirits of the camp had gone down with the barometer. The men were more than ever conscious of their bad luck, and having only themselves to blame for persistently remaining at Thompson's Flat, were ready to cast the guilt of their folly on the nearest available scapegoat. Monty was accustomed to entering the room unnoticed, but on the present occasion he saw that instead of contemptuously ignoring his presence, the other occupants of the saloon were unmistakably scowling at him. Scarcely had he made his timid way to his accustomed seat when Big Simpson said in a loud voice:

"Gentlemen, have you noticed that our luck has been more particularly low down ever since that there beauty in the corner had the cheek to sneak in among us?"

"That's so!" exclaimed Slippery Jim. "Monty is ugly enough to spoil the luck of a blind nigger."

"You see," continued Simpson, "thishyer beauty is like the Apostle Jonah. While he was aboard ship there wasn't any sort of luck, and at last the crew took and hove him overboard, and served him right. There's a mighty lot of wisdom in the Scriptures if you only take hold of 'em in the right way. My dad was a preacher, and I know what I'm talking about."

"That's more than the rest of us does," retorted Slippery Jim. "We ain't no ship's crew and Monty ain't no apostle. If you mean we ought to heave him into the creek, why don't you say so?"

"It wouldn't do him any harm," replied Simpson. "He's a dirty beast, and this camp hasn't no call to associate with men that's afraid of water, except, of course, when it comes to drinking it."

"I'm as clean as any man here," said Monty, stirred for the moment to indignation. "Mining ain't the cleanest sort of work, and I don't find no fault with Simpson nor any other man if he happens to carry a little of his claim around with him."

"That'll do," said Simpson severely. "We don't allow no such cuss as you to make reflections on gentlemen. We've put up with your ugly mug altogether too long, and I for one ain't going to do it no longer. What do you say, gentlemen?" he continued, turning to his companions, "shall we trifle with our luck, and lower our self-respect any longer by tolerating the company of that there disreputable, low-down, miserable coyote? I go for boycotting him. Let him work his own claim and sleep in his own cabin if he wants to, but don't let him intrude himself into this saloon or into our society anywhere else."

The proposal met with unanimous approval. The men wanted something on which to wreak their spite against adverse fortune, and as Monty was unpopular and friendless he was made the victim. Simpson ordered him to withdraw from the saloon and never again to enter it at an hour when other gentlemen were there. "What's more," he added, "you'll not venture to speak to anybody; and if any gentleman chances to heave a remark at you you'll answer him at your peril. We're a law-abiding camp, and we don't want to use violence against no man; but if you don't conform to the kind and reasonable regulations that I've just mentioned to you, there'll be a funeral, and you'll be required to furnish the corpse. You hear me?"

"I hear you," said Monty. "I hear a man what's got no more feelings than a ledge of quartz rock. What harm have I ever done to any man in the camp? I know I ain't handsome, but there's some among you that ain't exactly Pauls and Apolloses. If you don't want me here why don't you take me and shoot me? It would be a sight kinder and more decent than the way you say you mean to treat me."

"Better dry up!" said Simpson, warningly. "We don't want none of your lip. We've had enough of you, and that's all about it."

"I've no more to say," replied Monty, rising and moving to the door. "If you've had enough of me I've had enough of you. I've been treated worse than a dog, and I ain't going to lick no man's hand. Good evening, gentlemen. The day may come when some of you will be ashamed of this day's work, that is if you've heart enough to be ashamed of anything."

So saying Monty walked slowly out, closing the door ostentatiously behind him. His departure was greeted by a burst of laughter, and the cheerfulness of the assembled miners having been restored by the sacrifice of Monte Carlo, a subdued gaiety once more reigned in the saloon.

Monty returned to his desolate cabin, and after lighting his candle threw himself into his bunk. The man was coarse and ig-norant, but he was capable of keenly feeling the insult that had been put upon him. He knew that he was hideously ugly, but he had never dreamed that the fact would be made a pretext for thrusting him from the society of his kind. Strange to say he felt little anger against his persecutors. No thoughts of revenge came to him as he lay in the silence and loneliness of his cabin. For the time being the sense of utter isolation crowded out all other sen-sations. He felt infinitely more alone when the sound of voices reached him from the saloon than he would have felt had he been lost in the great North forest.

Before coming to Thompson's Flat he had lived in one of the large towns of Michigan, where decent and civilized people had not been ashamed to associate with him. Here, in this wretched mining camp, a gang of men, guiltless of washing, foul in lan-guage, and brutal in instinct, had informed him that he was unfit to associate with them. There had never been any one among the miners for whom he had felt the slightest liking; but it had been a comfort to exchange an occasional word with a fellow-being. Now that he was sentenced to complete isolation he felt as a shipwrecked man feels who has been cast alone on an uninhab-ited island. If the men would only retract their sentence of ban-ishment, and would permit him to sit in his accustomed corner of the saloon he would not care how coarsely they might insult him — if only he could feel that his existence was recognized.

But no! There was no hope for him. The men hated him be-cause of his maimed and distorted face. They despised him, pos-sibly because he did not permit himself to resent their conduct with his revolver, and thus give them an excuse for killing him. He could not leave the camp and make his way without supplies to the nearest civilized community. There was nothing for him to do but to work his miserable claim, and bear the immense and awful loneliness of his lot. As Monty thought over the situation and saw the hopelessness of it, his breath came in quick gasps until he broke into a sob, and the tears flowed down his scarred and grimy cheeks.

A low, inquiring mew drew his attention for a moment from

his woes. The camp cat — a ragged, disreputable animal, who owned no master, and rejected all friendly advances — stood in the door of Monty's cabin, with an interrogative tail pointing to the zenith and a friendly arch in his shabby back.

Monty had often tried to make friends with the cat, but Tom had repulsed him as coldly as the miners themselves. Now in his loneliness the man was glad to be spoken to, even by the camp cat; and he called it to him, though without any expectation that the animal would come to him. But Tom, stalking slowly into the cabin, sprang after a moment's hesitation into Monty's bunk, and purring loudly in a hoarse voice, as one by whom the accomplishment of purring had long been neglected, gently and tentatively licked the man's face, and kneaded his throat with two soft and caressing paws. A vast sob shook both Monty and the cat. The man put his arms around the animal, and hugging him closely, kissed his head. The cat purred louder than ever, and presently laying his head against Monty's cheek, he drew a long breath and sank into a peaceful slumber.

Monty was himself again. He was no longer alone. Tom, the cat, had come to him in the hour of his agony and had brought the solace of a love that did not heed his ugliness. Henceforth he would never be wholly alone, no matter how strictly the men might enforce their boycott against him. He no longer cared what they might do or say. He felt the warm breath of the friendly animal on his cheek. The remnant of its right ear twitched from time to time and tickled his lip. The long sinewy paws pressed against his neck trembled nervously, as the cat dreamed of stalking fat sparrows, or of stealing fried fish. Its hoarse croupy purr sounded like the sweetest music to the lonely man. "There's you and me, and me and you, Tom!" said Monty, stroking the cat's ragged and crumpled fur. "We'll stick together, and neither of us won't care a cuss what them low-down fellows says or does. You and me'll be all the world to one another. God bless you forever for coming to me this night."

From that time onward, Monte Carlo and Tom were the most intimate of friends. Wherever the man went the cat followed. When he was working in the shallow trench, where the sparse gold dust was found, Tom sat or slept on the edge of the trench, and occasionally reminded Monty of the presence of a friend, by the soft crooning sound which a mother cat makes to her newborn kittens. The two shared their noon meal together; and it was said by those who professed to have watched them that the cat always had the first choice of food, while the man contented himself with what his comrade rejected. In the evening Monty and Tom sat together at the door of the cabin, and conversed in low tones of any subject that happened to interest them for the time being. Monty set forth his political and social views, and the cat, listening with attention, mewed assent, or more rarely expressed an opposite opinion by the short, sharp mew, or an unmistakable oath.

Once or twice a week Monty was compelled to visit the saloon for groceries and other necessities. He always made these visits when the men of the camp were working in their claims; and he was invariably accompanied by Tom, who trotted by his side, and sprang on his shoulder while he made his purchases. The saloon keeper declared that when once by accident he gave Monty the wrong change, Tom loudly called his friend's attention to the error and insisted that it should be rectified. "That there cat," said the saloon keeper to his assembled guests on the following evening, "ain't no ordinary cat, for it stands to reason that if he was he wouldn't chum with Monty. A cat that takes up with such a pal, and that talks pretty near as well as you or me, or any other Christian is, according to what I learned at Sunday School, possessed with the devil. You mark my word, Monty sold his soul to that pretended cat, and presently he'll be shown a pocket chuck full of nuggets, and will go home with his ill-gotten gains while we stay here and starve."

The feeling that there was something uncanny in the relations that existed between Monte Carlo and the cat gradually spread through the camp. While no man condescended to speak to the boycotted Monty, a close watch was kept upon him. Slippery Jim asserted that he had heard Monty and Tom discuss the characters of nearly every man in the camp, while he was concealed one evening in the tall grass near Monty's cabin.

"First," said Jim, "Monty asked kind o' careless like, 'What may be your opinion of that there Big Simpson?' The cat, he just swears sort of contemptuous, and then Monty says, 'Jest so! That's what I've always said about him; and I calculated that a cat of your intelligence would say the same thing.' By and by Monty says, 'What's that you're saying about Red-haired Dick? You think he'd steal mice from a blind cat, and then lay it on the dog? Well! my son! I don't say he wouldn't. He's about as mean as they make 'em, and if I was you I wouldn't trust him with a last year's bone!' Then they kept on jawing to each other about this and that, and exchanging views about politics and religion, till after a while Tom lets out a yowl that sounded as if it was meant for a big laugh. Monty, he laughed too; and then he says, 'I never thought you would have noticed it, but that's exactly what Slippery Jim does every time he gets a chance.'

"I don't know," continued Jim, "what they were referring to, but I do know that Monty and the cat talk together just as easy as you and me could talk, and I say that if it's come to this, that we're going to allow an idiot of a man and a devil of a cat to take away the characters of respectable gentlemen, we'd better knuckle down and beg Monty to take charge of this camp and to treat us like so many Injun squaws."

Other miners followed Slippery Jim's example, in watching and listening to his conversations with the cat, and the indignation against the animal and his companion grew deep and bitter. It was decided that the scandal of an ostentatious friendship between a boycotted man and a cat that was unquestionably possessed by the devil must be ended. The suggestion that the cat should be shot would undoubtedly have been carried out, had it not been that Boston, who was a spiritualist, asserted that the animal could be hit only by a silver bullet. The camp would gladly have expended a silver bullet in so good a cause, but there was not a particle of silver in the camp, except what was contained in two or three silver watches.

After several earnest discussions of the subject it was resolved that the cat should be hung on a stout witch-hazel bush, growing within a few yards of Simpson's cabin. It was recognized that hanging was an eminently proper method of treatment in the case of a cat of such malevolent character; and as for Monty himself, more than one man openly said that if he made any trouble about the disposal of the cat, he would instantly be strung up to a convenient pine tree which stood close to the witch-hazel bush.

The next morning a committee of six, led by Big Simpson, cautiously approached the trench in which Monty was working. There was nearly an eighth of a mile between Monty's claim and those of the other miners. The latter had taken possession of that part of Thompson's Flat which seemed to hold out the best promise for gold, and Monty, partly because of his unprepossessing appearance, had been compelled to content himself with what was considered to be the least valuable claim in the camp.

The committee made its way through the long coarse grass, which had sprung up under the fierce heat of summer, and was already as parched and dry as tinder. They had intended to seize the cat before Monty had become aware of their presence; and they were somewhat disconcerted when Monty, with the cat clasped tightly in his arms, came running towards them. "There's Injuns just over there in the woods," he cried. "Tom sighted them first, and after he'd called me I looked and see three devils sneaking along towards your end of the camp. You boys, rush and get your Winchesters, and I'll be with you in a couple of minutes."

The men did not stop to question the accuracy of Monty's story. They forgot their designs against the cat, and no longer thought of their promise to shoot the boycotted man if he ventured to address them. They ran to their cabins, and seizing their rifles, rallied at the saloon, which was the only building capable of affording shelter. It was built of stout logs, and its one door was immensely thick and strong. By firing through the windows the garrison could keep at bay, at least for a time, the cautious Indian warriors, who would not charge through the open, so long as they could harass the miners from the shelter of the wood.

After Monty had placed his cat in his bunk he took his rifle, and carefully closing the door of his cabin, joined his late enemies in the saloon. Several of them nodded genially to him as he entered, and Simpson, who was arranging the plan of defence, told him to take a position by one of the rear windows. The men understood perfectly well that Monty's warning had saved them from a surprise in which they would have been cruelly massacred. Perhaps they felt somewhat ashamed of their previous treatment of the man, but they offered no word of apology.

However Monty thought little of their manner. Although he knew that in all probability the siege would be prolonged until not a single miner was left alive, his thoughts were not on himself or his companions. Would the Indians overlook his cabin, or in case they found it, would they offer violence to Tom? These were the questions that occupied his mind as he watched through the window for the gleam of a rifle barrel in the edge of the forest and answered every puff of smoke with an instantaneous shot from his Winchester. The enemy kept carefully under cover, and devoted their efforts to firing at the windows of the saloon. Already three shots had taken effect. Two dead bodies lay on the floor, and a wounded man sat in the corner, leaning against the wall, and slowly bleeding to death. Suddenly a cloud of smoke shot up in the direction of Monty's cabin. The Indians had set fire to the dry grass, and the flames were sweeping towards the cabin in which the cat was imprisoned.

Monty took in the situation and came to a decision with the same swiftness and certainty with which he pulled the trigger. "You'll have to excuse me, boys, for a few minutes," he said, rising from his crouched attitude and throwing his rifle into the hollow of his arm.

"What's the matter with you?" growled Simpson. "Have you turned coward all of a sudden, or are you thinking of scaring the Injuns by giving them a sight of your countenance?"

"That there cabin of mine will be blazing inside of five minutes, and I've left Tom in it with the door fastened," replied Monty, ignoring the insulting suggestions of Simpson, and beginning to unbar the door.

"Here! Come back, you blamed lunatic!" roared Simpson. "Do you call yourself a white man, and then throw your life away for a measly, rascally cat?"

"I am going to help my friend if I kin," said Monty. "He stood by me when thishyer camp throwed me over, and I'll stand by him now he's in trouble."

So saying he quietly passed out and vanished from the sight of the astonished miners.

"I told you," said Slippery Jim, "that Monty was bewitched by that there cat. Who ever heard of a man that was a man who cared whether a cat got burned to death or not?"

"You shut up!" exclaimed Simpson. "You haven't got sand enough to stand by your own brother — let alone standing by a cat."

"What's the matter with you?" retorted Jim. "You was the one who proposed boycotting Monty, and now you're talking as if he was a tin saint on wheels."

"Monty's acted like a man in this business," replied Simpson, "and it's my opinion that we've all treated him pretty particular mean. If we pull through this scrimmage Monty's my friend, and don't you forget it."

Monte Carlo lost none of his habitual caution, although he was engaged in what he knew to be a desperate and nearly hopeless enterprise. On leaving the saloon he threw himself flat on the ground, and slowly drew himself along until he reached the shelter of the high grass. Then rising to his hands and knees he crept rapidly and steadily in the direction of his cabin.

His course soon brought him between the fire of the miners and that of the Indians, but as neither could see him he fancied he was safe for the moment. He was drawing steadily closer to his goal, and was already beginning to feel the thrill of success, when a sharp blow on the right knee brought him headlong to the ground. A stray shot, fired possibly by some nervous miner who had taken his place at the saloon window, had struck him and smashed his leg.

He could no longer creep on his hands and knees, but with

indomitable resolution he dragged himself onward by clutching at the strong roots of the grass. His disabled leg gave him exquisite pain as it trailed behind him, and he knew that the wound was bleeding freely; but he still hoped to reach his cabin before faintness or death should put a stop to his progress. He felt sure that the shot which had struck him had not been aimed at him by an Indian, for if it had been he would already have felt the scalping knife. The nearer he drew to his cabin the less danger there was that the Indians would perceive him. If he could only endure the pain and the hemorrhage a few minutes longer he could reach and push open the door of his cabin, and give his imprisoned friend a chance for life. He dragged himself on with unfaltering resolution, and with his silent lips closed tightly. Not a groan nor a curse nor a prayer escaped him. He stuck to his task with the grim fortitude of the wolf who gnaws his leg free from the trap. All his thoughts and all his fast-vanishing strength were concentrated on the effort to save the creature that had loved him.

After an eternity of anguish he reached the open space in front of the cabin, where the thick smoke hid him completely from the sight of both friends and foes. The flames had just caught the roof, and the heat was so intense that for an instant it made him forget the pain of his wound, as his choked lungs gasped for air. The wail of the frightened animal within the cabin gave him new energy. Digging his fingers into the ground he dragged himself across the few yards that separated him from the door. He reached it at last, pushed it open, and with a smile on his face lost consciousness as the cat bounded out and fled like a mad creature into the grass.

Two hours later a troop of Mounted Police, who had illegally and generously crossed the border in time to drive off the Indians and to rescue the few surviving members of the camp, found, close to the smouldering embers of Monty's cabin, a scorched and blackened corpse, by the side of which sat a bristling black cat. The animal ceased to lick the maimed features of the dead man, and turned fiercely on the approaching troopers. When one of them dismounted and attempted to touch the corpse the cat flew at him with such fury that he hurriedly remounted his horse,

amid the jeers of his comrades. The cat resumed the effort to recall the dead man to life with its rough caresses, and the men sat
silently in their saddles watching the strange sight.

"We can't bury the man without first shooting the cat," said
one of the troopers.

"Then we'll let him lie," said the sergeant in command. "We
can stop here on our way back from the Fort, and maybe by that
time the cat'll listen to reason. I'd as soon shoot my best friend as
shoot the poor beast now."

And the troop passed on, leaving Tom alone in the wilder-
ness with his silent friend.

William Livingston Alden.

THE QUEEN'S CAT

Once there was a great and powerful King who was as good as gold and as brave as a lion, but he had one weakness, which was a horror of cats. If he saw one through an open window he shuddered so that his medals jangled together and his crown fell off; if any one mentioned a cat at the table he instantly spilled his soup all down the front of his ermine; and if by any chance a cat happened to stroll into the audience chamber, he immediately jumped on to his throne, gathering his robes around him and shrieking at the top of his lungs.

Now this King was a bachelor and his people didn't like it; so being desirous of pleasing them, he looked around among the neighbouring royal families and hit upon a very sweet and beautiful princess, whom he asked in marriage without any delay, for he was a man of action.

Her parents giving their hearty consent, the pair were married at her father's palace; and after the festivities were over, the King sped home to see to the preparation of his wife's apartments. In due time she arrived, bringing with her a cat. When he saw her mounting the steps with the animal under her arm, the King, who was at the door to meet her, uttering a horrid yell, fell in a swoon and had to be revived with spirits of ammonia. The courtiers hastened to inform the Queen of her husband's failing, and when he came to, he found her in tears.

"I cannot exist without a cat!" she wept.

"And I, my love," replied the King, "cannot exist with one!"

"You must learn to bear it!" said she.

"You must learn to live without it!" said he.

"But life would not be worth living without a cat!" she wailed.

"Well, well, my love, we will see what we can do," sighed the King.

"Suppose," he went on, "you kept it in the round tower over

there. Then you could go to see it."

"Shut up my cat that has been used to running around in the open air?" cried the Queen. "Never!"

"Suppose," suggested the King again, "we made an enclosure for it of wire netting."

"My dear," cried the Queen, "a good strong cat like mine could climb out in a minute."

"Well," said the King once more, "suppose we give it the palace roof, and I will keep out of the way."

"That is a good scheme," said his wife, drying her eyes.

And they immediately fitted up the roof with a cushioned shelter, and a bed of catnip, and a bench where the Queen might sit. There the cat was left; and the Queen went up three times a day to feed it, and twice as many times to visit it, and for almost two days that seemed the solution of the problem. Then the cat discovered that by making a spring to the limb of an overhanging oak tree, it could climb down the trunk and go where it liked. This it did, making its appearance in the throne-room, where the King was giving audience to an important ambassador. Much to the amazement of the latter, the monarch leapt up screaming, and was moreover so upset, that the affairs of state had all to be postponed till the following day. The tree was, of course, cut down; and the next day the cat found crawling down the gutter to be just as easy, and jumped in the window while the court was at breakfast. The King scrambled on to the breakfast table, skilfully overturning the cream and the coffee with one foot, while planting the other in the poached eggs, and wreaking untold havoc among the teacups. Again the affairs of state were postponed while the gutter was ripped off the roof, to the fury of the head gardener, who had just planted his spring seeds in the beds around the palace walls. Of course the next rain washed them all away.

This sort of thing continued. The wistaria vine which had covered the front of the palace for centuries, was ruthlessly torn down, the trellises along the wings soon followed; and finally an ancient grape arbour had perforce to be removed as it proved a sure means of descent for that invincible cat. Even then, he cleverly utilized the balconies as a ladder to the ground; but by this time the poor King's nerves were quite shattered and the doctor was called in. All he could prescribe was a total abstinence from cat; and the Queen, tearfully finding a home for her pet, composed herself to live without one. The King, well cared for, soon revived and was himself again, placidly conducting the affairs of state, and happy in the society of his beloved wife. Not so the latter.

Before long it was noticed that the Queen grew wan, was often heard to sniff, and seen to wipe her eyes, would not eat, could not sleep, — in short, the doctor was again called in.

"Dear, dear," he said disconsolately, combing his long beard with his thin fingers. "This is a difficult situation indeed. There must not be a cat on the premises, or the King will assuredly have nervous prostration. Yet the Queen must have a cat or she will pine quite away with nostalgia."

"I think I had best return to my family," sobbed the poor Queen, dejectedly. "I bring you nothing but trouble, my own."

"That is impossible, my dearest love," said the King decidedly — "Here my people have so long desired me to marry, and now that I am at last settled in the matrimonial way, we must not disappoint them. They enjoy a Queen so much. It gives them something pretty to think about. Besides, my love, I am attached to you, myself, and could not possibly manage without you. No, my dear, there may be a way out of our difficulties, but that certainly is not it." Having delivered which speech the King lapsed again into gloom, and the doctor who was an old friend of the King's went away sadly.

He returned, however, the following day with a smile tangled somewhere in his long beard. He found the King sitting mournfully by the Queen's bedside.

"Would your majesty," began the doctor, turning to the Queen, "object to a cat that did not look like a cat?"

"Oh, no," cried she, earnestly, "just so it's a *cat*!"

"Would your majesty," said the doctor again, turning to the King, "object to a cat that did not look like a cat?"

"Oh, no," cried he, "just so it doesn't *look* like a cat!"

"Well," said the doctor, beaming, "I have a cat that is a cat and that doesn't look any more like a cat than a skillet, and I should be only too honoured to present it to the Queen if she would be so gracious as to accept it."

Both the King and the Queen were overjoyed and thanked the doctor with tears in their eyes. So the cat — for it was a cat though you never would have known it — arrived and was duly presented to the Queen, who welcomed it with open arms and felt better immediately.

It was a thin, wiry, long-legged creature, with no tail at all, and large ears like sails, a face like a lean isosceles triangle with the nose as a very sharp apex, eyes small and yellow like flat buttons, brown fur short and coarse, and large floppy feet. It had a voice like a steam siren and its name was Rosamund.

The King and Queen were both devoted to it; she because it was a cat, he because it seemed anything but a cat. No one indeed could convince the King that it was not a beautiful animal, and he had made for it a handsome collar of gold and amber — "to match," he said, sentimentally, "its lovely eyes." In sooth so ugly a beast never had such a pampered and luxurious existence, certainly never so royal a one. Appreciating its wonderful good fortune, it never showed any inclination to depart; and the King, the Queen, and Rosamund lived happily ever after.

Peggy Bacon.

CALVIN

Calvin is dead. His life, long to him, but short for the rest of us, was not marked by startling adventures, but his character was so uncommon and his qualities were so worthy of imitation, that I have been asked by those who personally knew him to set down my recollections of his career.

His origin and ancestry were shrouded in mystery; even his age was a matter of pure conjecture. Although he was of the Maltese race, I have reason to suppose that he was American by birth as he certainly was in sympathy. Calvin was given to me eight years ago by Mrs. Stowe, but she knew nothing of his age or origin. He walked into her house one day out of the great unknown and became at once at home, as if he had been always a friend of the family. He appeared to have artistic and literary tastes, and it was as if he had inquired at the door if that was the residence of the author of *Uncle Tom's Cabin*, and, upon being assured that it was, had decided to dwell there. This is, of course, fanciful, for his antecedents were wholly unknown, but in his time he could hardly have been in any household where he would not have heard *Uncle Tom's Cabin* talked about. When he came to Mrs. Stowe, he was as large as he ever was, and apparently as old as he ever became. Yet there was in him no appearance of age; he was in the happy maturity of all his powers, and you would rather have said in that maturity he had found the secret of perpetual youth. And it was as difficult to believe that he would ever be aged as it was to imagine that he had ever been in immature youth. There was in him a mysterious perpetuity.

After some years, when Mrs. Stowe made her winter home in Florida, Calvin came to live with us. From the first moment, he fell into the ways of the house and assumed a recognized position in the family, — I say recognized, because after he became known he was always inquired for by visitors, and in the letters to the other members of the family he always received a message. Although the least obtrusive of beings, his individuality always made itself felt.

His personal appearance had much to do with this, for he

was of royal mould, and had an air of high breeding. He was large, but he had nothing of the fat grossness of the celebrated Angora family; though powerful, he was exquisitely proportioned, and as graceful in every movement as a young leopard. When he stood up to open a door — he opened all the doors with old-fashioned latches — he was portentously tall, and when stretched on the rug before the fire he seemed too long for this world — as indeed he was. His coat was the finest and softest I have ever seen, a shade of quiet Maltese; and from his throat downward, underneath, to the white tips of his feet, he wore the whitest and most delicate ermine; and no person was ever more fastidiously neat. In his finely formed head you saw something of his aristocratic character; the ears were small and cleanly cut, there was a tinge of pink in the nostrils, his face was handsome, and the expression of his countenance exceedingly intelligent — I should call it even a sweet expression if the term were not inconsistent with his look of alertness and sagacity.

It is difficult to convey a just idea of his gaiety in connection with his dignity and gravity, which his name expressed. As we know nothing of his family, of course it will be understood that Calvin was his Christian name. He had times of relaxation into utter playfulness, delighting in a ball of yarn, catching sportively at stray ribbons when his mistress was at her toilet, and pursuing his own tail, with hilarity, for lack of anything better. He could amuse himself by the hour, and he did not care for children; perhaps something in his past was present to his memory. He had absolutely no bad habits, and his disposition was perfect. I never saw him exactly angry, though I have seen his tail grow to an enormous size when a strange cat appeared upon his lawn. He disliked cats, evidently regarding them as feline and treacherous, and he had no association with them. Occasionally there would be heard a night concert in the shrubbery. Calvin would ask to have the door opened, and then you would hear a rush and a "pestzt," and the concert would explode, and Calvin would quietly come in and resume his seat on the hearth. There was no trace of anger in his manner, but he wouldn't have any of that about the house. He had the rare virtue of magnanimity. Although he had fixed notions about his own rights, and extraordinary persistency in getting them, he never showed temper at a repulse; he simply and firmly persisted till he had what he wanted. His diet was one point; his idea was that of the scholars about dictionaries, — to "get the best." He knew as well as any one what was in the house, and would refuse beef if turkey was to be had; and if there were oysters, he would wait over the turkey to see if the oysters would not be forthcoming. And yet he was not a gross gourmand; he would eat bread if he saw me eating it, and thought he was not being imposed on. His habits of feeding, also, were refined; he never used a knife, and he would put up his hand and draw the fork down to his mouth as gracefully as a grown person. Unless necessity compelled, he would not eat in the kitchen, but insisted upon his meals in the dining-room, and would wait patiently, unless a stranger were present; and then he was sure to importune the visitor, hoping that the latter was ignorant of the rule of the house, and would give him something. They used to say that he preferred as his table-cloth on the floor a certain well-known church journal; but this was said by an Episcopalian. So far as I know, he had no religious prejudices, except that he did not like the association with Romanists. He tolerated the servants, because they belonged to the house, and would sometimes linger by the kitchen stove; but the moment visitors came in he arose, opened the door, and marched into the drawing-room. Yet he enjoyed the company of his equals, and never withdrew, no matter how many callers — whom he recognized as of his society — might come into the drawing-room. Calvin was fond of company, but he wanted to choose it; and I have no doubt that his was an aristocratic fastidiousness rather than one of faith. It is so with most people.

The intelligence of Calvin was something phenomenal, in his rank of life. He established a method of communicating his wants, and even some of his sentiments; and he could help himself in many things. There was a furnace register in a retired room, where he used to go when he wished to be alone, that he always opened when he desired more heat; but never shut it, any more than he shut the door after himself. He could do almost everything but speak; and you would declare sometimes that you could see a pathetic longing to do that in his intelligent face. I have no desire to overdraw his qualities, but if there was one thing in him more noticeable than another, it was his fondness for nature. He could content himself for hours at a low window, looking into the ravine and at the great trees, noting the smallest stir there; he delighted, above all things, to accompany me walking about the garden, hearing the birds, getting the smell of the fresh earth, and rejoicing in the sunshine. He followed me and gambolled like a dog, rolling over on the turf and exhibiting his delight in a hundred ways. If I worked, he sat and watched me, or looked off over the bank, and kept his ear open to the twitter in the cherry-trees. When it stormed, he was sure to sit at the window, keenly watching the rain or the snow, glancing up and down at its falling; and a winter tempest always delighted him. I think he was genuinely fond of birds, but, so far as I know, he usually confined himself to one a day; he never killed, as some sportsmen do, for the sake of killing, but only as civilized people do, — from necessity. He was intimate with the flying-squirrels who dwell in the chestnut-trees, — too intimate, for almost every day in the summer he would bring in one, until he nearly discouraged them. He was, indeed, a superb hunter, and would have been a devastating one, if his bump of destructiveness had not been offset by a bump of moderation. There was very little of the brutality of the lower animals about him; I don't think he enjoyed rats for themselves, but he knew his business, and for the first few months of his residence with us he waged an awful campaign against the horde, and after that his simple presence was sufficient to deter them from coming on the premises. Mice amused him, but he usually considered them too small game to be taken seriously; I have seen him play for an hour with a mouse, and then let him go with a royal condescension. In this whole matter of "getting a living," Calvin was a great contrast to the rapacity of the age in which he lived.

I hesitate a little to speak of his capacity for friendship and the affectionateness of his nature, for I know from his own reserve that he would not care to have it much talked about. We understood each other perfectly, but we never made any fuss about it; when I spoke his name and snapped my fingers, he came to me; when I returned home at night, he was pretty sure to be waiting for me near the gate, and would rise and saunter along the walk, as if his being there were purely accidental, — so shy was he commonly of showing feeling; and when I opened the door he never rushed in, like a cat, but loitered, and lounged, as if he had had no intention of going in, but would condescend to. And yet, the fact was, he knew dinner was ready, and he was bound to be there. He kept the run of dinner-time. It happened sometimes, during our absence in the summer, that dinner would be early, and Calvin walking about the grounds, missed it and came in late. But he never made a mistake the second day. There was one thing he never did, — he never rushed through an open doorway. He never forgot his dignity. If he had asked to have the door opened, and was eager to go out, he always went deliberately; I can see him now, standing on the sill, looking about at the sky as if he was thinking whether it were worth while to take an umbrella, until he was near having his tail shut in.

His friendship was rather constant than demonstrative. When we returned from an absence of nearly two years, Calvin welcomed us with evident pleasure, but showed his satisfaction rather by tranquil happiness than by fuming about. He had the faculty of making us glad to get home. It was his constancy that was so attractive. He liked companionship, but he wouldn't be petted, or fussed over, or sit in any one's lap a moment; he always extricated himself from such familiarity with dignity and with no show of temper. If there was any petting to be done, however, he chose to do it. Often he would sit looking at me, and then, moved by a delicate affection, come and pull at my coat and sleeve until he could touch my face with his nose, and then go away contented. He had a habit of coming to my study in the morning, sitting quietly by my side or on the table for hours, watching the pen run over the paper, occasionally swinging his tail round for a blotter, and then going to sleep among the papers by the ink-stand. Or, more rarely, he would watch the writing from a perch on my shoulder. Writing always interested him, and, until he understood it, he wanted to hold the pen.

He always held himself in a kind of reserve with his friend, as if he had said, "Let us respect our personality, and not make a 'mess' of friendship." He saw, with Emerson, the risk of degrading it to trivial conveniency. "Why insist on rash personal relations with your friend?" "Leave this touching and clawing." Yet I would not give an unfair notion of his aloofness, his fine sense of the sacredness of the me and the not-me. And, at the risk of not being believed, I will relate an incident, which was often repeated. Calvin had the practice of passing a portion of the night in the contemplation of its beauties, and would come into our chamber over the roof of the conservatory through the open window, summer and winter, and go to sleep on the foot of my bed. He would do this always exactly in this way; he never was content to stay in the chamber if we compelled him to go upstairs and through the door. He had the obstinacy of General Grant. But this is by the way. In the morning, he performed his toilet and went down to breakfast with the rest of the family. Now, when the mistress was absent from home, and at no other time, Calvin would come in the morning, when the bell rang, to the head of the bed, put up his feet and look into my face, follow me about when I rose, "assist" at the dressing, and in many purring ways show his fondness, as if he had plainly said, "I know that she has gone away, but I am here." Such was Calvin in rare moments.

He had his limitations. Whatever passion he had for nature, he had no conception of art. There was sent to him once a fine and very expressive cat's head in bronze, by Frémiet. I placed it on the floor. He regarded it intently, approached it cautiously and crouchingly, touched it with his nose, perceived the fraud, turned away abruptly, and never would notice it afterward. On the whole, his life was not only a successful one, but a happy one. He never had but one fear, so far as I know: he had a mortal and a reasonable terror of plumbers. He would never stay in the house when they were here. No coaxing could quiet him. Of course he didn't share our fear about their charges, but he must have had some dreadful experience with them in that portion of his life which is unknown to us. A plumber was to him the devil, and I have no doubt that, in his scheme, plumbers were foreordained to do him mischief.

In speaking of his worth, it has never occurred to me to estimate Calvin by the worldly standard. I know that it is customary now, when any one dies, to ask how much he was worth, and that no obituary in the newspapers is considered complete without such an estimate. The plumbers in our house were one day overheard to say that, "They say that *she* says that *he* says that he wouldn't take a hundred dollars for him." It is unnecessary to say that I never made such a remark, and that, so far as Calvin was concerned, there was no purchase in money.

As I look back upon it, Calvin's life seems to me a fortunate one, for it was natural and unforced. He ate when he was hungry, slept when he was sleepy, and enjoyed existence to the very tips of his toes and the end of his expressive and slow-moving tail. He delighted to roam about the garden, and stroll among the trees, and to lie on the green grass and luxuriate in all the sweet influences of summer. You could never accuse him of idleness, and yet he knew the secret of repose. The poet who wrote so prettily of him that his little life was rounded with a sleep, understated his felicity; it was rounded with a good many. His conscience never seemed to interfere with his slumbers. In fact, he had good habits and a contented mind. I can see him now walk in at the study door, sit down by my chair, bring his tail artistically about his feet, and look up at me with unspeakable happiness in his handsome face. I often thought that he felt the dumb limitation which denied him the power of language. But since he was denied speech, he scorned the inarticulate mouthings of the lower animals. The vulgar mewing and yowling of the cat species was beneath him; he sometimes uttered a sort of articulate and well-bred ejaculation, when he wished to call attention to something that he considered remarkable, or to some want of his, but he never went whining about. He would sit for hours at a closed window, when he desired to enter, without a murmur, and when it was opened he never admitted that he had been impatient by "bolting" in. Though speech he had not, and the unpleasant kind of utterance given to his race he would not use, he had a mighty power of purr to express his measureless content with congenial society. There was in him a musical organ with stops of varied power and expression, upon which I have no doubt he could have performed Scarlatti's celebrated cat's-fugue.

Whether Calvin died of old age, or was carried off by one of the diseases incident to youth, it is impossible to say; for his departure was as quiet as his advent was mysterious. I only know that he appeared to us in this world in his perfect stature and beauty, and that after a time, like Lohengrin, he withdrew. In his illness there was nothing more to be regretted than in all his blameless life. I suppose there never was an illness that had more of dignity and sweetness and resignation in it. It came on gradually, in a kind of listlessness and want of appetite. An alarming symptom was his preference for the warmth of a furnace-register to the lively sparkle of the open wood-fire. Whatever pain he suffered, he bore it in silence, and seemed only anxious not to obtrude his malady. We tempted him with the delicacies of the season, but it soon became impossible for him to eat, and for two weeks he ate or drank scarcely anything. Sometimes he made an effort to take something, but it was evident that he made the effort to please us. The neighbours — and I am convinced that the advice of neighbours is never good for anything — suggested catnip. He wouldn't even smell it. We had the attendance of an amateur practitioner of medicine, whose real office was the cure of souls, but nothing touched his case. He took what was offered, but it was with the air of one to whom the time for pellets was passed. He sat or lay day after day almost motionless, never once making a display of those vulgar convulsions or contortions of pain which are so disagreeable to society. His favourite place was on the brightest spot of a Smyrna rug by the conservatory, where the sunlight fell and he could hear the fountain play. If we went to him and exhibited our interest in his condition, he always purred in recognition of our sympathy. And when I spoke his name, he looked up with an expression that said, "I understand it, old fellow, but it's no use." He was to all who came to visit him a model of calmness and patience in affliction.

I was absent from home at the last, but heard by daily postal-card of his failing condition; and never again saw him alive. One sunny morning, he rose from his rug, went into the conservatory (he was very thin then), walked around it deliberately, looking at all the plants he knew, and then went to the bay-window in the dining-room, and stood a long time looking out upon the little field, now brown and sere, and toward the garden, where perhaps the happiest hours of his life had been spent. It was a last look. He turned and walked away, laid himself down upon the bright spot in the rug, and quietly died.

It is not too much to say that a little shock went through the neighbourhood when it was known that Calvin was dead, so marked was his individuality; and his friends, one after another, came in to see him. There was no sentimental nonsense about his obsequies; it was felt that any parade would have been distasteful to him. John, who acted as undertaker, prepared a candle-box for him, and I believe assumed a professional decorum; but there may have been the usual levity underneath, for I heard that he remarked in the kitchen that it was the "dryest wake he ever attended." Everybody, however, felt a fondness for Calvin, and regarded him with a certain respect. Between him and Bertha there existed a great friendship, and she apprehended his nature; she used to say that sometimes she was afraid of him, he looked at her so intelligently; she was never certain that he was what he appeared to be.

When I returned, they had laid Calvin on a table in an upper chamber by an open window. It was February. He reposed in a candle-box, lined about the edge with evergreen, and at his head stood a little wine-glass with flowers. He lay with his head tucked down in his arms, — a favourite position of his before the fire, — as if asleep in the comfort of his soft and exquisite fur. It was the involuntary exclamation of those who saw him, "How natural he looks!" As for myself, I said nothing. John buried him under the twin hawthorn-trees, — one white and the other pink, — in a spot where Calvin was fond of lying and listening to the hum of summer insects and the twitter of birds.

Perhaps I have failed to make appear the individuality of character that was so evident to those who knew him. At any rate, I have set down nothing concerning him but the literal truth. He was always a mystery. I did not know whence he came; I do not know whither he has gone. I would not weave one spray of falsehood in the wreath I lay upon his grave.

Charles Dudley Warner.